OTHER
*Harlequin Romances*
by MARGARET ROME

Many of these titles are available at your local bookseller, or through the Harlequin Reader Service.

For a free catalogue listing all available Harlequin Romances, send your name and address to:

HARLEQUIN READER SERVICE,
M.P.O. Box 707, Niagara Falls, N.Y. 14302
Canadian address: Stratford, Ontario, Canada.

or use order coupon at back of book.

# THE GIRL AT EAGLES' MOUNT

by

## MARGARET ROME

HARLEQUIN BOOKS

TORONTO
WINNIPEG

Original hard cover edition published in 1971
by Mills & Boon Limited, 17-19 Foley Street,
London W1A 1DR, England

© Margaret Rome 1971

SBN 373-01676-X

Harlequin edition published April 1973

# CHAPTER ONE

'No, begorrah, I will not accept it! Never will I believe a Rooney capable of such treachery!' Michael Rooney's face betrayed apoplectic rage as he drew himself up to his full height of five feet six inches—that looked less because of his rotundness—and glared across the paper-littered desk at his calm, composed niece, Georgina.

For a few seconds, she continued with her task of sorting through the pile of letters that occupied her attention. Rapidly she glanced over each one and scribbled notes in individual margins so as to enable her highly competent secretary to compose the kind of reply expected of Electronic International—American manufacturers of copper foil for use in computers—of which she was a co-director. Michael's ire increased with each second he was ignored. His eyes began to bulge as suppressed rage forced up the level of his blood pressure, causing the veins in his forehead to knot alarmingly. Georgina sighed, pushed aside her papers, and looked up just in time to prevent him from exploding. Coolly she reached for a cigarette and lighted it, resigning herself to listening, yet again, to another repetition of the story she had heard so many times before, and especially during the past months, from her uncle.

To forestall him, she decided to declare her intention once more, forcibly, so that he might be finally convinced of her determination to carry out the plan she had outlined to him; the plan to which he was so vehemently objecting.

'The factory,' she elucidated clearly with a faint American accent, 'is to be built here, in the north-west of England.' When her uncle would have burst into excited argument, she waved him to silence and stated firmly, 'It has been decided, Uncle Michael, finally, irrevocably! I won't listen to another word about the Emerald Isle and its wonderful people. The factory,' she stabbed downward with her index finger to emphasize her point, 'will be built right here!'

Michael Rooney's face crumpled like a child's. His hand groped backward, seeking a chair and, when he found one, he sank down despondently and stared at her determined face with unbelieving eyes. 'You *can't* mean that, Georgina,' he faltered, his rage subsiding into utter dismay. 'Not when you know how deep our family's roots are in Irish soil. Remember the stories your father told you when you were a child about your grandfather, Seamus Rooney, who left Ireland as a boy because there was no work available and went to seek a better life in America. And of how, after marrying your grand-mother, he found his feet and began to prosper. In many ways he loved the land of his adoption, but it never took the place of Ireland. He loved Erin, as he called it, so much that that love was passed down through the family, together with his one bright, burning hope. You *know* what it was he hoped for, Georgina. He dreamt of returning to Ireland and the people he loved. He wanted to play a small part

6

in helping the country's economy by transferring part of his business there, so creating employment for the families of those with whom he had spent his boyhood. He died before realizing his dream and so, too, did your father, but surely,' he half rose from his chair and entreated her, 'surely, now, when that dream could become reality, you don't intend simply to ignore his wish? How can you consider building a factory here, in England, when you know you would be destroying an ideal cherished throughout two generations by the people to whom you owe the prosperity and prestige you and your mother enjoy so much today?'

Georgina snorted; no other word could do justice to the contemptuous sound. 'Sentimental claptrap, Uncle Michael! How many times do I have to repeat: there is no place for sentiment in business.' She went on hardly, 'As you already know, two sites have been tentatively approved for our new branch; one here, the other in Ireland. This present location is ideally suited to our needs, so there's no sense in wasting valuable time by going over to Ireland to examine the proposed site there. Here we have been promised every facility and we know we will be able to choose our workers from an ample labour force. Public authorities are falling over themselves to grant our every wish. In a nutshell, Uncle Michael, this site is tailor-made to our requirements, so I've no intention of even considering Ireland, nor its feckless, lackadaisical inhabitants with their reputation of never doing today what can be put off until tomorrow. I have a business to run, a highly competitive business, and I simply can't afford to carry passengers. Not even passengers who've kissed the Blarney stone and have a shamrock tucked behind each ear!'

'Blasphemy!' Michael roared when she stopped for breath. He was dancing with rage, his anger so great that after one initial retort he was rendered incoherent. Georgina thought as she watched him that, although American born and bred, he was more Irish than the Irish. Fanatically patriotic, fiery-tempered, garrulous, and occasionally slightly tipsy, but for all that, heart-meltingly charming when he chose to be, which, she thought cynically, was usually when he wanted something he could not have.

She accelerated his already boiling temper to flash-point by leaning negligently against her desk and proceeding to blow smoke rings into the air with an air of being prepared to wait until he should manage to control his unruly emotions. Michael, his ego offended by the way she was keeping full command of the situation, resentfully eyed her, deploring the way her black hair was scraped back from her face into a sleek roll at the back of her head—to his mind, a woman's hair should form a soft frame for her face and not look as if it were sculptured. Also, he disliked the severely tailored suit, without a ribbon or frill in sight, that gave her a definite touch-me-not look—perfect it might be for giving an aura of businesslike efficiency, but death to any young man's hopes of a sly cuddle. But most of all he was offended by the look of amusement in her clear grey eyes; amusement afforded by himself, and he was huffed by it. Belligerently, he voiced his opinions aloud.

'Sentiment? You don't know the meaning of the word! You're a cold, unfeeling young woman playing about in a man's world! Where's your femininity, girl? Where are the soft, human touches a man expects from his womenfolk? You're like a mechanical doll with a computer where your heart should be: a perfect replica of your mother, in fact!'

Her head jerked up. Complacently aware that his shot had found its mark, he carried on loudly. 'Yes, *your mother!* The woman who was responsible for my brother's death as surely as if she'd pushed him under the car that ran him over. He would have been happier married to an iceberg! Do you want to finish up like her? Handsome, upright, a terrific businesswoman, but with an empty heart—and empty arms!'

A sudden weakness swept over Georgina, causing her uncle's angry face to fade into a grey mist and then to advance waveringly back into focus. She put out a groping hand to clutch at a bottle of pills that lay on her desk. She waited, her uncle's continuing tirade washing over her, until she felt able to walk steadily towards the washbasin in the corner of the room to fill a glass with water. Michael raged on, unnoticing, while she quickly swallowed a couple of pills and drank thirstily from the glass. With as much nonchalance as she could muster, she walked over to the window and willed her rebellious body back to normal. These attacks were becoming too frequent. Frighteningly so. The doctor she had consulted in New York might have been right when he had diagnosed overwork and strain. How she had

9

laughed at his suggestion that she should give herself a chance to recover by having a long holiday. She *never* took holidays. They were a complete waste of time.

Once again Michael's remarks began to register. He was repeating himself in his over-excited Irish way, the words tumbling over themselves in an agitated splutter '... cold, heartless woman ... killed my brother with her icy disdain ... empty heart ... empty arms.' Something snapped inside Georgina's head and she whipped around on him with an anger that more than equalled his own.

'And have you heard the tales that have been told by the women of our family, Uncle? No? Then let me enlighten you, but before I do you'd better sit down, you're in for a shock!'

Bewildered, he obeyed her command, too stunned by the fury in her eyes to do otherwise. She leant with one hand on either side of his chair and lashed out the words. 'If it were not for the women of this family there would be no business! Grandmother told my mother this, and she passed it on to me, but only, I might add, after having lived through a bitter experience which proved my grandmother's words to be true.' As she drew a deep breath Michael sat open-mouthed. 'Grandfather had a fine brain and he used it to his best advantage when he chose an American bride. After inventing the process his business was founded on, he sat back on his haunches and allowed his wife to seek out the markets and to bring in the orders. Grandmother wore the soles from umpteen pairs of shoes in her quest for interested buyers—and eventually found them. It's she that both you and my father had to thank for the thriving business you inherited, not your happy-go-lucky father!'

Michael tried to protest, but she squashed him. 'History repeated itself in the case of my father and mother. Another charming Irishman; another businesslike American wife. Did you ever ask yourself, Uncle Michael, what my father was doing in that disreputable neighbourhood on the day he was killed? He had been visiting one of his many women-friends and had imbibed a little too freely of the "hard stuff". In other words, he wasn't pushed under that car by my mother or anyone else—he was blind drunk!'

Michael slumped down in his chair, defeated. He had heard nothing he did not already know, but his refusal to face realities had allowed him to push the facts to the back of his mind until, as the years softened his memory, he could have believed they had never been. He flinched as she hammered home her advantage.

'And what about you, Uncle Michael? What did you do with your life? You were unfortunate because you had no wife to act as a crutch. You opted for taking your share of the business in hard cash, leaving my father in full control, then you frittered it away on one hare-brained scheme after another until you were broke to the wide and had to prevail upon my mother to give you a job. And yet you have the *gall*,' her voice shook with indignation, 'to call her names!'

He did not attempt to answer. Her dagger had plunged deep; her verbal thrusts had completely annihilated him. She looked down at his grey face and felt a stir of compassion. When she was a child she had idolized both her father and his equally inconsequential brother. Children don't seek beneath the surface; they seldom search for hidden depths, and Michael and Brendan Rooney had both had an ample supply of surface charm with which to woo a gullible child. But a little of the regard she had felt for him still lingered and brought with it a sense of shame at her savage ripping to shreds of all that remained of his pride. She lifted her hand to give him a tentative shake—his immobility was unnatural—but as she leant forward the grey haze swept back across her eyes with a suddenness that made her gasp. Her head began to swim and as the grey cloud darkened to black she called out childishly, *'Uncle Mike!'* He opened his arms just in time to catch her as she fell.

Astonishment was his primary emotion, quickly followed by panicky concern when he realized that his slightly disdainful, irritatingly headstrong young niece was, for the first time in her life, utterly dependent upon him. Her boneless immobility as he gathered her up in his arms alarmed him only slightly less than the fragile weightlessness that registered itself as he carried her towards a leather settee placed under the window. For a second after setting her down, he searched her white face with anguished eyes, willing the black crescent lashes to lift from over her misty-grey eyes. It mattered nothing that those same eyes would probably fill with annoyance or hauteur at the sight of him; her untimely collapse had forced home to him the reality that the regard he felt for his brother's child had not diminished over the years as he had imagined, but was still there, a strong, clannish feeling of partisanship. Emotion reared up inside him until it was a lump in his throat. Their harsh words and differences were submerged under a wave of compassion as he watched her lying there, the ultra-modern guise she wore like an armour stripped away leaving her looking, in her unconscious state, like a defenceless child.

Inwardly, even while he made renewed efforts to rouse her, he railed angrily against his sister-in-law, Stella Rooney, for allowing such a thing to happen to her only child. Why wasn't she here, looking after her as a mother should, instead of sitting behind a desk in her New York office issuing orders to men who, Michael opined, deserved to be horsewhipped for their spineless acceptance of her petticoat tyranny? Nothing Georgina had said in her mother's defence had softened Michael's animosity towards the woman his brother had married. To him, she had always shown a hard front, an unsympathetic coldness which his warm Irish nature recoiled against. It was unnatural, he had told himself years ago, for any woman to be so completely aloof and withdrawn as she had invariably been each time Brendan had invited him around to share a meal. Granted, those occasions had been the climax of chance meetings that had resulted in their joining forces for an almighty binge, but what woman of flesh and blood could deny two brothers the right to exchange a few drinks and reminiscences now and then? And now this. Not content with manipulating her husband into an early grave, she was forcing the yoke of big business on to the shoulders of a young girl who should, by rights, have no greater worry than that of deciding which boyfriend she should choose to bestow her favours upon.

Alarmed by his niece's lack of response to his efforts to revive her, Michael swore under his breath and reached over to thrust an imperative finger on the buzzer on her desk. In the ensuing seconds while he waited for his call to be answered, he frowned helplessly down at Georgina's waxen face and invoked the help of the Irish saints while he angrily vowed: *No*, Stella Rooney, you won't get away with the same thing a second time. I don't know how I'll stop you, but, begorrah, I *will* stop stop you!

Susan Chesterman, Georgina's secretary, rushed into the room, her notebook at the ready, in response to the prolonged buzzing. She stopped just inside of the door and gave a horrified gasp when she saw Georgina laid out on the settee with Michael, his unruly grey hair standing on end, bending over her. Not surprisingly, having been an unwilling eavesdropper on many rows between Michael and his niece, she immediately jumped to the wrong conclusion. Dropping her notebook, she ran towards the settee screaming:

'*Mr Rooney, what have you done?*'

But before Michael could begin his explanation, another voice reached across the room, the authoritative, demanding voice of Cassell D. Whalley, a young executive in whom Stella had such great confidence that she had designated him Georgina's right-hand man for the duration of time they would be involved in setting up the new factory. Michael detested him. He embodied everything he most disliked in the younger generation Americans; brashness, intolerance of age, conceit, and determination to climb to the top whosoever's neck he had to stand on. Grudgingly, he had to admit that Cassell D. Whalley was nobody's fool. He was fully aware that he had entered into a probationary period and that, if he made good, his success was assured. Michael was also well acquainted with the fact that Cassell D. Whalley considered him to be an old fool whose presence in the firm was as superfluous as were —he had once outspokenly stated—the outrageous ideas with which he tried to brainwash his niece. The animosity between the two was almost physical.

'I think, Rooney,' Cassell D. Whalley accused curtly, 'you've overreached yourself this time.' Without bothering to listen to Michael's splutter of indignant explanation, he waved Susan towards the phone:

'Get a doctor, quickly, then get this old idiot out of here or I won't be responsible for my actions!'

Ignoring Michael's bellow of rage, he moved towards Georgina and began to pat her lightly on the cheek, calling her name insistently. 'Georgie, waken up, d'you hear me? Georgie!'

Michael shook off Susan's detaining hand when he saw his niece stir and heard her give a soft, long-drawn-out sigh. His worry-lined face relaxed into a smile of relief when he heard her murmur, but drew back immediately into a scowl when he heard

15

the whispered words, 'Wally darling, don't look so worried, I'll be fine in a minute, just fine.'

*Wally darling!* So that was the way the wind blew! Michael hunched up his shoulders and withdrew before he could again be ignominiously dismissed. Deep in thought, he wandered into his own office and sat down to wait. But he had no real need to wait for the doctor's verdict; far too often in the past he had seen grown men fall by the wayside stricken with the same look of strain and exhaustion he had seen on his niece's face earlier. Those men had been like rats on a treadmill, for ever striving for faster and better results. Some of them had been intelligent enough to realize that they were getting nowhere, but had been too afraid or too fascinated to jump off; they had carried on, convinced that the pile of money they were greedily acquiring represented all that was best in life. Michael sighed for them. Never had they known the joy that was to be found in a solitary walk across soft, springy peat on a beautiful spring morning, or the aesthetic pleasure of casting a fly across a sparklingly clear lough to capture one of the myriad brown-speckled trout that skimmed tantalizingly near the surface. Lost in memories, he was back again in Ireland where, to echo his niece's words, he had squandered his share of the family fortune on one hare-brained scheme after another. Perhaps she was right, but at least in the County of Kerry, the home of his forebears, where he had spent his inheritance, he would be remembered by some with affection and by others with gratitude.

Suddenly his drooping shoulders straightened

and his clouded blue eyes shone with the light of inspiration. A telegram, that was all that would be needed! A telegram could be the forerunner of a life of freedom for his niece and—he almost jigged out of his chair as he grew wildly optimistic—perhaps some freedom for others, too!

# CHAPTER TWO

MICHAEL found it incredibly easy to carry out his plan of action; perhaps it was that the luck of the Irish, which had seemed to desert him so often in the past, was now working for him, because every effort he made towards his goal was rewarded by a successful conclusion. The prompt reply which he received to his telegram was the first boost to his morale, and in the days that followed he carried it around with him as a talisman, patting it now and then to give himself confidence whenever his courage wavered.

For three days Georgina was shut away in her bedroom, heavily sedated. The doctor had been quite adamant that she was to have no visitors and Michael kicked his heels outside of her room until finally he managed to waylay the doctor as he left after one of his early morning visits.

'Doctor,' he grabbed his arm when he would have passed by, 'I must have a word with you. I'm Michael Rooney, Georgina's uncle.'

'Well, Mr Rooney, what is it you wish to know?' The doctor sounded constrained; Michael quickly summed him up as an overworked G.P. with no time to spare for pleasantries, so he did not prevaricate.

'I don't need to ask you what's wrong with my niece, Doctor,' Michael's aged gamin face puckered into worry lines. 'All I need to know is how long it will be before I can get her away from this perpetual round of business? You must be aware that unless that girl is removed from this environment she'll collapse completely. I'm the only relative she has in this country, so I intend to exercise my prerogative and take over her life for a while,' he breathed in deeply, 'whether she likes it or not! So if you can tell me when she'll be fit to travel, I'll arrange to get her away from her blasted business long enough to teach her how to really live.'

'Hm.' As the doctor deliberated his eyes wandered thoughtfully over Michael, taking in the bag at the knees of his trousers, the socks that were not even remotely matching, and the violently hued tie that fought a losing battle with his square-checked shirt—then he smiled.

'Mr Rooney, you are the only person in this establishment who hasn't pestered me to allow my patient to talk business. Will today be soon enough . . .?'

Michael's face lightened with relief and his hand shot out to grasp the doctor's in a handshake that communicated his brimming thankfulness. Huskily he asked: 'Just one more thing, Doctor.' The doctor's eyebrows rose in enquiry. 'Can we keep this between ourselves? I'd like, if possible, to get her away without fuss or argument.'

He gave Michael the flicker of a smile and replied obliquely, 'I have a very tight schedule planned, Mr Rooney, so it's possible I might not manage to fit in another visit to your niece today. I've left orders that she has not to be disturbed, but that's because I want to keep those vultures off her back.

The pills I've prescribed will keep her drowsy and relaxed during the journey, but I'll have to trust you to see to it that she is as little upset as possible while she's travelling.' With a swift nod that told Michael he was now on his own, the doctor turned on his heel and strode swiftly towards the lift.

Michael expelled a breath of relief; the ease with which his biggest problem had been resolved was almost frightening. As he moved towards Georgina's room his step had a jauntiness that betrayed his rising spirits—nothing could go wrong now—the luck of the Irish was with him!

Georgina's gentle breathing was the only sound to be heard as he tiptoed into her room. He looked down with compassion at the white oval of her face, serene in sleep, but, even allowing for the gloom caused by shaded windows, too tragically white, then he moved quietly towards the cupboard where he knew her cases were stacked. Delicately he eased one of them from the pile and set it down on the floor before heading towards the closet that held her clothes. He looked in utter confusion at the variety of tailored suits and dresses that hung there, then with a masculine shrug of helplessness, he grasped the handful that were nearest and put them on the floor beside the case. Next he scooped up dainty wisps of underwear from the drawers, hoping with momentary embarrassment that she would not question his clumsy nosing into her private possessions, then he added to these some jumpers and a couple of pairs of shoes and crammed the lot into the suitcase with soundless, desperate haste. When the locks were snapped shut, beads of sweat stood out like tears on his broad brow and he eased the tie from around his constricted throat before preparing to sidle into the corridor with his burden. Again he was fortunate, not a soul in sight, and in a couple of seconds he was back in his own room. As he poured himself a stiff whiskey, his hands shook. 'Glory be, Rooney,' he berated himself angrily, 'you'd never make an espionage agent! What if someone *had* caught you sneaking out with Georgina's clothes, the worst they could have done would be shoot you!' Then, with a jubilant return of confidence, he lifted his glass and toasted: *'Erin go bragh!'* before tossing the drink down his parched throat.

At breakfast he received more good news. The hotel was a quiet one, small but comfortable, and the management had been only too eager to allow themselves to be taken over by Electronic International for the duration of their stay because at that time of the year, early May, business was not brisk. Willingly, they had allocated unused bedrooms to be used as temporary offices and one of the downstairs rooms as a boardroom-cum-reception room in which to receive visiting businessmen. As a result of such confined living, it was inevitable that everyone should eat together. Michael sat down in his usual place, sharing a table with Cassell Whalley and Susan Chesterman, with Georgina's empty chair as a reminder of her absence. They had almost reached the end of the meal when Cassell Whalley broke his moody silence to inform him:

'Rooney, I've sent a cable to Stella informing her of Georgie's illness, but they can't contact her at

Head Office. She set off on a business trip, but didn't leave any forwarding address—you know how she hates to be bothered with mail or telephone messages when she's on the road. Anyway, Head Office say the best they can do is to let her know immediately she gets back. But meanwhile,' he glowered across the table at Michael, obviously laying the blame for the setback squarely upon him, 'there are a thousand and one decisions to be made and no one with enough authority to sign the necessary papers to enable the deal to go through.'

Michael assumed an expression of bland sympathy which he hoped would hide the effervescent surge of hope that surged through his veins. Georgina's health was his first consideration, but with her removal from the scene, and Stella's absence, no further move could be made to finalize the arrangements to build the factory in England. There was hope yet! He made a noise in his throat which passed for a murmur of commiseration, but Cassell Whalley's stabbing eyes were full of suspicion when they swung towards him. 'Don't you go living in hope, Rooney,' he sneered with an assurance born of his growing relationship with Georgina. 'Your pipe-dream of an Irish factory is as far away as it ever was, and if all Irishmen are as unbusinesslike as you I'm sure glad of it.' He swivelled towards Susan with a broad grin. 'D'you know what I was told the other day? I was told that when you cross the Shannon at Athlone you have to throw away your watch and buy a calendar! And that's the country,' he spluttered, 'where this guy wants us to build our factory, can you imagine . . .?'

Susan obviously could not, because she burst into a peal of mocking laughter. Michael sat, inwardly fuming, but outwardly impervious to their scornful amusement. He waited until they were calmer, then rose with what he hoped was a dignified bow and departed in silence. His ears burned when, as he mounted the stairs, he heard a fresh outburst of laughter, but he gritted his teeth and kept a firm hold on his temper. 'I hope you'll laugh when you discover we've gone, ye spalpeens,' he gritted, 'but I'll bet it'll be nearer to tears you'll be!' But his rage subsided as a satisfying thought presented itself: his absence from lunch and dinner would be put down to a fit of sulks, and by the time they got around to searching for him he and Georgina would be well on their way to Ireland.

As he set about finalizing his arrangements, Michael for once truly appreciated the power that money can command. The hire-car firm he telephoned promised him a chauffeur-driven limousine to drive them to the nearest airport and said they would arrange for a similar one to be waiting at Dublin airport to take them from there to Kerry. Air reservations presented no problem, it was too early in the year for heavy booking, so he had no trouble in obtaining two seats on that day's flight. All that was now left to do was to get Georgina prepared for the journey. Whalley, he knew, had a business appointment in town to which he was taking Susan, so he sat in the lounge with his eyes glued to the window until he saw them both drive off before hurrying up to Georgina's room.

She had not stirred. He walked over to the bed and gave a loud cough as a preliminary to wakening her, but still she slumbered on, deeply asleep. There was nothing else for it but to rouse her physically. Feeling utterly heartless, he grasped her by the shoulders and shook her gently.

'Georgina, wake up!' She gave a moan of dissent and turned to settle on her side. He tried again. 'Georgina, can you hear me? You must waken up, mavourneen, there's something terribly important that we must do!' She dragged open her heavy lids and gazed with grey-eyed wonder into his perspiring face.

'G'away, Uncle Mike,' she yawned childishly, 'go away, I want to sleep.'

'No, you mustn't,' he shook her again vigorously in his urgency. 'You must get up and dress immediately. It's imperative'—he suddenly had a brainwave—'it's imperative that you attend a meeting in town in fifteen minutes or your plans for the factory won't go through!'

He had to admire her indomitable spirit. When his words penetrated her fogged brain, she bravely struggled into a sitting position and fought to throw off the stupor caused by the sedatives.

'Very well, hand me some clothes, please, Uncle,' she agreed, meek with weariness. 'I'll take a shower before I dress.'

Hastily he did as she asked, then, when she had disappeared unsteadily into the bathroom, he danced a jig of delight. When the door closed behind her slight figure, he dashed out of the room and down the corridor to his own bedroom. Swiftly he grabbed their luggage—her suitcase and his own —and hurried down the stairs to the small foyer. Even as he set them down, he heard the swish of tyres outside on the gravel drive and a second later a uniformed chauffeur entered through the open doorway. Michael beamed a welcome and handed him the suitcases. 'My niece will be down in a couple of minutes,' he told him.

The man touched his cap respectfully. 'I hope she won't be longer than a few minutes, sir, it's quite a drive to the airport and we don't want to be late for take-off.'

The very idea of this sent Michael scurrying back to Georgina's room. To his relief, he saw she was almost ready, but when she tried to take a step towards him her knees buckled under her and she would have fallen if he had not reached out to support her.

Peevishly she pleaded: 'Can't Wally attend to whatever has to be done, Uncle Mike? I ... I'm afraid I'm feeling most peculiar.' She made a move towards the bed as if drawn there by a magnet, but Michael forestalled her intention to lie down by grabbing her arm and urging her towards the door.

'Don't worry, you'll feel fine once you're out in the open air, I promise you. Just you lean on me until you feel stronger.'

Strangely acquiescent, she obeyed him until they had negotiated the stairs and walked outside to the car where the chauffeur was waiting to help Michael to install her in the luxurious rear seat. For all of ten seconds after they had driven away Michael held his breath, expecting some last-minute hitch to foil his plan, but nothing did. When the hotel had disappeared from view he looked around at Georgina and a smile of happiness relaxed his tense face when he saw her snuggled up, sound asleep, looking the picture of contentment.

Michael was grateful that this intermittent drowsiness lasted all during the flight. There was no delay at the airport. The chauffeur, who had been put in the picture regarding her illness, helped Michael to get her aboard the aircraft and after a few disjointed questions, to which Michael gave what must have been satisfactory answers, she settled her head against the comfortably padded seat and went back to sleep.

It was not until he saw the coastline of England disappear from sight that Michael felt completely safe—even self-congratulatory. The most hazardous part of the undertaking was now behind him, he was on his way to friends in the country he regarded as his homeland. Whatever ructions he would have to face—and he had no doubt that there would be some when Georgina recovered—would all be worth while. He began to feel he had pulled off a magnificent coup, one that would not have disgraced the Sinn Fein itself. As his natural ebullience asserted itself he began conveniently to subdue his complex of guilt until, by the time the plane was hovering over Dublin, he was convinced that far from being annoyed by his high-handedness, his niece would be overjoyed—might even feel indebted to him—for his clever handling of her affairs.

When the plane touched down he managed to

rouse her sufficiently to disembark, but he had to half carry her towards the car which, much to his relief, he saw was waiting. Without demur, she settled into the back while he went to collect their luggage, and it was no surprise to him when he returned to find her once again sleeping soundly. He pondered on whether or not to delay just long enough to have a meal before setting off on the long journey to Kerry, but decided against it. She had shown no interest in the food offered on the plane and if he were foolish enough to insist upon rousing her to eat her return to full consciousness could jeopardize all his arrangements. So he climbed in beside the chauffeur and instructed him to drive away.

They drove for hours, and not once during the journey did Georgina emerge long enough from her stupor to enjoy the delightful scenery and the sight of the many scattered smallholdings and tiny cottages they passed along their route. Many times Michael was tempted to waken her, loath to miss sharing with her her first sight of landmarks and beauty spots familiar to her by name only since early childhood. But discretion overruled these impulses and he contented himself with the assurance that, beautiful though they might be, the sights she was missing did not compare half so well as those she was about to enjoy during her stay in the County of Kerry.

So they journeyed on through Kildare, and Leix, Tipperary and Limerick, until when dusk was falling they crossed the Kerry boundary where mountains began to rise above the gentle slopes of hills and the salty tang of the sea was borne along on the freshening breeze that blew straight from the Atlantic Ocean. Onward they sped, along straight, deserted roads, always climbing, until at last through the darkness a light became visible and Michael sighed with satisfaction.

'We've arrived,' he told the chauffeur. 'That light ahead shines from Eagles' Mount.'

Georgina stirred, aware of her uncle's voice, and tried to puzzle out what she was doing stretched out in the back of a car, but for some reason her brain would not function well enough to supply the answer. She wrinkled her forehead as she battled with worrying thoughts and a strange sense of foreboding that was sending alarm signals to her sluggish brain. Then she became aware of hunger, but just as she was about to address a demand for food to her uncle the car jerked to a halt and she heard a man welcoming Michael in a charmingly warm and lilting accent. A few words were exchanged before the car was again opened and an onrush of cold air set her shivering.

'Quickly,' the voice said, 'let's get her into the house before she catches a chill.' She felt herself lifted bodily in a pair of strong, gentle arms and held closely against a steadily beating heart while she was carried into the house and up some stairs; all the time with her dark head nestling against the stranger's broad chest. She heard his voice again as he laid her down on something soft. It said: 'Kate, will you get her into bed, please, and see that she has something hot to drink?'

Kind hands undressed her and tucked warm bedclothes under her chin, but although she wanted to repay the owner of those hands by drinking the soup she later pleaded with her to accept, she was far too tired to make the effort.

# CHAPTER THREE

WHEN she awoke the next morning and looked dazedly around the alien room, Georgina thought for a terrifying few seconds that she had gone out of her mind. A dozen vague, conflicting impressions teased her memory. *Had* she been in a plane? Why, upon awakening, had she expected to find herself in the back of a speeding car? Her last clear recollection was of a row with her uncle, but after that— blankness. But no, there *was* something else! She remembered a strong pair of arms holding her so confidently she had felt immediately secure, and a voice, a firm, low-toned voice with a lilting accent: an Irish accent!

She jerked upright, suddenly wide awake, as the implication struck her. She remembered more Irish voices, a woman's—her name was Kate—but the others she could put no name to except that of her uncle whose accent always thickened the nearer he travelled towards Ireland: last night his words had been spoken in an almost unintelligible brogue! She leapt out of the old-fashioned canopied bed to run across to the window, but staggered the last few steps when a wave of lightheadedness swept over her. Gasping with alarm, she clutched at the heavy curtains that cloaked the window and with a supreme effort managed to drag the cumbersome things open wide. Her worst fears were confirmed. Framed by the enormous windowpanes was a view with certain rare qualities of its own which she knew could belong to only one country in the world; and one county. Hundreds of times she had heard described the rise and fall of the grass-smothered hill she saw far in the distance to her left, and the opalescent lake that nestled beneath them and changed its colour with the mood of the sky. To her right were boulder-strewn mountains that she knew harboured the king of birds—the eagle—along their jagged crests. As she looked down, she felt as an eagle must as it scrutinized the countryside from its lofty eyrie. The house clung high up on the side of a cliff; its rocky face fell from beneath her window to disappear into the turmoil of ocean that frothed and surged around its base. Rocks, detached no doubt from the mass untold years before, formed a grasping claw that stretched out skeleton fingers into the boiling sea, and the soughing wind caught up among dark clefts and deep fissures joined the angry cawing of circling sea-birds in a discordant lament which made her draw back, repelled.

A sound from behind caused her to swing around so suddenly that she almost overbalanced and she clutched at the heavy curtains to steady herself while her frightened eyes searched the room for its source.

'Good gracious me, alannah!' The old woman who entered set down the tray she was carrying and hastened over to her. 'You shouldn't be out of your bed, at all, at all.' She took hold of Georgina's arm and urged her firmly forward. 'Himself'll have the hide off me if you should catch a chill in his own house after having come all the way from England!'

'Himself?' Georgina's confused mind grasped at this piece of information and clamoured for more.

The old woman nodded vigorously. 'To be sure, it was Himself who carried you up here in his own arms last night, and it was he who told me: "Look after her, Kate," and that's just what I'm about to do. So get back into bed, bairn, and get this breakfast inside of ye before it starts to stick to the plate with starvation.'

The smell of crisply fried bacon drifting from the tray reminded Georgina that she was ravenous, so without further demur she obeyed Kate's order, tell-herself that after she had eaten would be a better time to start demanding answers to the questions that burned on her tongue.

Kate kept vigil by the bed, determined to see that every scrap was eaten, and while Georgina tucked into the satisfying meal she covertly studied her gaoler. She could have been any age from sixty to ninety. Her face was stamped with lines of endur-ance, but her fine, soft skin was devoid of wrinkles until she smiled. Then, when her mouth lifted up-wards, scores of laughter lines appeared with such involuntary swiftness that one was aware that only many years of such exercise could effect such in-delible results. She was amply built, with generous bust and hips, but her hands were coarse and red-dened with many years of service, although, judging from her soft humming as she waited patiently for Georgina to finish her meal, her life of servility had caused her no bitterness. Her age, Georgina decided, could best be guessed by her mode of dress: voluminous skirts that swept right down to the tops of her high-laced shoes, and a light shawl crossed over the bosom of a prim blouse fastened at the neck with a brooch made up of a scrawl of fine rolled-gold wire fashioned into the word Mother.

No one, Georgina decided, could fear the wearer of such a badge of maternal devotion, and she warmed towards her. 'Tell me, Kate, what am I doing here in this house?'

Kate looked her astonishment. 'Why, your uncle, Michael Rooney, brought you here to convalesce after your nasty illness, don't you know?' Her shrewd eyes took in the enormity of Georgina's smoke-grey eyes in her pale pointed face and a trace of annoyance crossed her face. ''Tis the wisest thing that young spalpeen has ever done, I'll wager. There's no finer air than ours for building up an ailing body, and you look as if you need plenty of it, alannah. Has your family no eyes that they missed seeing how poorly you were before you reached this state?' She clicked her teeth and, without waiting for an answer, reached over for the now empty tray. 'But never you mind,' she comforted as she rose to go, 'by the time you're ready to leave you'll be one of the bonniest colleens in all Ireland! Get you back to sleep now for another spell, then later, if you feel able, you can get up for an hour before lunch.'

Georgina's mouth opened to remonstrate, but then she changed her mind and settled back against her pillows. The food had done her good, she felt immensely refreshed and her mind was now beginning to function normally, but she needed strength for the battle which she foresaw would come when she demanded of her uncle that he take her straight back to England. So she took Kate's advice and snuggled down once more to rest.

A couple of hours later she awoke feeling fitter than she had done for months and more than ready to confront her Uncle Michael. When she swung out of bed and stood up, she was delighted to find that the weakness had gone from her limbs and the fuzziness from her head. She moved towards a door behind which she found a bathroom and to her satisfaction, when she turned on the taps the water was hot enough to allow her to bath. She wallowed in the old-fashioned tub, rejoicing in the softness of the water, then towelled dry and went back to her room to hunt out her clothes. Michael had forgotten nothing. She chose a soft blue jumper from the drawer of the tallboy and a cream-coloured skirt from the wardrobe. Shoes, tights, underwear, were all where one would expect to find them, and her brushes and combs were laid out on the wing-mirrored dressing-table. She took her time, enjoying the unaccustomed luxury of being free from pressure for what seemed to be the first time in her life, and sat idly brushing her black hair until it was smooth enough to be folded back into its usual pleat. Finally she felt ready to go downstairs. She moved towards the door, took a determined grasp of the handle, and strode out into the corridor to begin her search for Michael.

But when she stepped into the passageway her steps faltered. The bedroom had not prepared her for the massive proportions of the rest of the house. On either side of her the passage stretched high and silent until it faded into patches of intimidating gloom which her anxious eyes could not pierce. Faded, dusty tapestries lined the top half of the walls and sombre oak panels, black with age, continued down to the floor where threadbare carpeting failed to simulate warmth against the cold stone floor. High above, narrow glass-paned slits in the thick walls gave solitary access to watery sunlight that bravely filtered through, only to be dispersed before its feeble rays could lighten the darkness within. As she hesitantly moved down the passage a balustrade, indicating a staircase somewhere ahead, loomed in front of her, and when she found it and began to descend the shallow steps she heard the low sound of voices coming from below. When she reached the foot of the stairs she stared around at a great hall reminiscent of pictures she had seen of medieval castles in her school history books. It had many doors opening on to it, and as one of them was slightly ajar, she moved quietly towards it. The voices grew louder. Thankfully, she recognized her uncle's voice and she was just about to knock and enter the room when she heard him speak urgently.

'I tell you, Lian, this is a marvellous opportunity and one you mustn't overlook! I've tried—heaven knows how hard—to get her to listen to reason, but she's every bit as stubborn as her mother and as hard to convince. But you can do it if anyone can, I'm certain of that. All you need do is turn on the charm, give her a bit of the blarney, and before you know it she'll be eating out of your hand and Electronic International will be moving in to look for land for their new factory. What do you say, Lian, will you do it?'

Georgina froze with astonishment. She heard a low, amused laugh and then: 'But didn't you say, Rooney, that your niece is a hard-headed tycoon type with no time at all for sentiment or for any of the usual feminine pursuits? Wouldn't I be wasting my time trying to whisper sweet nothings into the ear of a ... how did you describe her? ... oh yes, a sexless computer!' More amused laughter, then the scrape of a chair against the floor as its occupant moved and began to walk towards the door. Filled with unreasonable panic, Georgina fled back towards the stairs and did not slow down until she had reached the sanctuary of her bedroom where, once inside, she held shaking hands up to her burning cheeks and began, with a sick sensation of betrayal, to dissect the incredible conversation. As she leant against the door feelings of anger, shame, and a very real sense of hurt washed over her. How could her uncle speak of her in such a derogatory way? Granted, they had had their disagreements, but always through her arguments and heated words had run a thread of affection she had thought was reciprocated. But now this! To actually encourage —no, exhort—this stranger to trick her into buying his useless land; and by such means! To flatter her, to play upon her emotions so that she might succumb to his so-called Irish charm to such an extent she would be willing to pour dollars into his empty coffers. She felt physically sick. Dully, she reflected that her mother had been right in her summing up of the Irish as a while and of the Rooney family in particular. As a child Georgina had been subjected often to her mother's biting indictment of their feckless and dilatory ways, but later, although she had outwardly tolerated her mother's forceful opinions, something inside of her had refused to accept that her lovable uncle was as worthless as her mother had so vehemently stated. She cringed away from examining in detail the worst hurt of all. She had had very little experience of men outside of the business world. Here again, her mother had been responsible. Her unhappy memories of her marriage to Brendan Rooney had been recounted so often and in such detail Georgina had subconsciously grown an armour of distrust with which she had unknowingly discouraged every budding suitor. All except Wally. Her shattered esteem recovered a little as she remembered his marked attentions; his solicitude and obvious admiration had culled up a growing affection that had flowered under the warmth of her mother's approval. Nothing concrete had been discussed between them, but Georgina knew that only pressure of business had prevented Wally from asking her to marry him.

With confidence partly restored by thoughts of Wally, she moved into action. Quietly angry, she began emptying the drawers of her belongings preparatory to packing her things and shaking the dust of Ireland from her feet. She would go back to the people she knew and understood, and perhaps in time, she would manage to forget the treachery her uncle had planned. But even as she snapped shut her suitcase a thought struck her. Why should such unprincipled rogues get away with their diabolical scheming? There were others, more gullible, who might be unfortunate enough to fall into their clutches, and it was not right that they should be left free to act out their confidence trick on some other unsuspecting soul.

Pensively she wandered over to the window to think. In business, one would first endeavour to gain the confidence of an unscrupulous opponent and then turn the tables upon him by denouncing him. The analytical brain her uncle so despised coolly marshalled her thoughts into a plan of action. Systematically, she tabulated her ideas until she was satisfied her plan would work, then with a cool smile she walked across to her suitcase and began to unpack.

She was so engrossed in her scheme that she failed to hear Kate enter the room; her surprised greeting was the first intimation she had of her presence.

'It's pleased I am to see you up and about, alannah. How are you feeling?'

Georgina swung round, startled. 'Oh, I'm feeling wonderfully fit, thank you, Kate. Fit enough,' she stated firmly, 'to lunch downstairs.'

Kate recognized that it would be futile to argue, and nodded her approval. 'Very well, I'll just go and tell Himself that he'll be having the pleasure of your company. Lunch is ready to be served, so I'll make haste and begin to dish up.'

Georgina followed her down into the hall and walked slowly towards the door Kate had indicated lead into the dining-room. When the old woman had bustled out of sight, she took a deep breath to harness the panic stirring inside of her before turning the knob and walking steadily into the room.

Immediately she was hailed by her uncle, who jumped to his feet at the sight of her. 'Georgina!' he clasped her hands in his, 'you're looking better already.'

Her mother would have approved of the way she began her offensive. Showing none of the rejected hurt his behaviour had caused her, she returned his greeting with a loving smile and advanced one step nearer her objective by answering. 'How could anyone help but feel better in such a wonderful place, Uncle Michael? I've never in my life seen a more breathtaking view, and this house ... ! Looking from my bedroom window I feel as if I'm perched high in an eagle's eyrie—an intoxicating sensation!'

'I'm glad you like the house, Miss Rooney,' the owner of the voice she had not been able to forget moved into view and stood smiling down at her. 'And how perceptive you are. The name of my house is Eagles' Mount. I'll be honoured if you will stay here as my guest for as long as you wish.'

Georgina lifted black lashes and stared upward into deep blue eyes that were dancing a message of welcome. Slowly, her eyes traversed the tall, lean length of him, noting the easy negligence with which he wore his ancient slacks and the rippling muscles that flexed visibly through the sleeves of a shabby, once expensive jacket. White, even teeth, a firmly cut mouth, and hair as black and unruly as any son of the devil's ought to be was her final summing up of the man she had pledged herself—was it a mere few minutes ago?—to hate! But no trace of animosity showed itself on the face she turned towards him, nor in her soft answer.

'How very generous of you, Mr ...?'

Michael jumped into the breach. Pleased astonishment that his seam of good luck had been extended to ensure his niece's willingness to stay in Ireland had kept him tongue-tied during the small interchange, but now the dam broke to let loose an excited introduction.

'Georgina, this is our host, Lian Ardulian, Chief of the Name!' This last was spoken with such proud reverence she found herself forced to look impressed. Her uncle then turned to the chief. 'And this, Lian, is my niece Georgina.'

Black rogue eyebrows lifted. 'Georgina!' he sounded surprisingly scornful. 'Never could I bring myself to employ such a masculine name to such a delectable piece of femininity! Do you mind,' his white smile flashed impudently, 'if I use the diminutive, Gina?'

She had to steel herself against the sudden onslaught of audacious charm. Her cool composure almost slipped as she recognized the powerful ammunition of her adversary, but she recovered quickly and, giving herself a mental shake, she forced her senses into order and threw herself into the part she intended to play. With a practised look of confused shyness, she stammered prettily:

'Why no, of course I don't mind, I think Gina sounds delightful.'

'And you will dispense with formality and call me, Lian?' he pressed.

'Very well ... Lian.' The blush this effort brought to her cheeks was not intended, but it seemed to please him, because his blue eyes took on a teasing

40

sparkle as he led her towards the table to begin the meal Kate was waiting to serve.

During lunch, Michael was content to merge into the background while Lian claimed her complete attention. Despite her contempt for the man, Georgina could not help but be fascinated as his low, lilting voice recounted some of the history of the house and of the wild doings of the first Chief of the Name who had led his followers into battle against many rival chiefs. His sorties had proved so successful he had conquered his way across the width of Ireland until he reached the western coast where, satisfied at last, he and his men had built themselves a fortress on the very edge of the Atlantic.

'Did you wonder, Gina, when you first saw it, why anyone should want to live in such a desolate spot?'

'You forget,' she answered, 'that all I've seen of the district is the view from my window. Is it *so* desolate?'

He nodded slowly, his expression growing momentarily sombre. 'Yes, I'm afraid so. Desolate enough to harbour the eagle from which the house takes its name. The bird is now almost extinct, except for a possible few that might still remain in some of the Scottish islands. Only here, where there is no industry, no traffic, no population to speak of, are they content to remain. Much as I enjoy their presence, I can but wish that things were different.'

'How different?' she probed, aware that she knew already the answer he would give. He drummed on the table with impatient fingers and brooded:

'I want to see life come to Ardulian! Life means

41

people; people need work and houses in which to live, they need recreation and transport to reach such places which, in turn, means new roads. Heaven forbid we should become a shambles of little square bungalows and ugly factory buildings, but it breaks my heart to see a place dying, with no inhabitants under sixty and all of *them* pining for the sons and daughters who have emigrated to other lands!'

She hid her triumph as he gazed down at the table, seemingly deep in disturbed thought. What an actor he was! If she had not overheard the conversation between himself and her uncle she might almost have been deceived into thinking he had the welfare of his people at heart, instead of the emptiness of his own pockets. Her indignation was hard to subdue and she answered him tartly.

'Nothing is achieved simply by wishing, and even if it were, wouldn't lack of endeavour diminish the value of the object gained?'

His head lifted in quick surprise at her note of censure and she could have kicked herself for her slip. Hurriedly she attempted to retrieve the situation by assuming an air of innocence and by reaching over to cover his tightly clenched fist with her hand.

'I can see you feel very strongly about the situation here, Lian, but I'm sure you have done everything possible for your people. How I wish there was something I could do to help!' She gazed up at him with a wistful sigh.

Immediately the shadows lifted from his eyes and his brooding look disappeared, leaving his face alive with pleasure. His firm brown hand uncurled its tenseness as he told her, 'You're so sweet, Gina, too sweet to be worried by my problems. I'm quite certain that if there were any way you could help you would do so, but as there isn't, let's drop the subject and find something more amusing to occupy you on your first day here.'

Georgina relaxed, her anxiety relieved, and strove to subdue the triumphant laughter that bubbled inside of her. If every day was to be as amusing as this one promised to be she was going to enjoy her holiday immensely!

# CHAPTER FOUR

AT dinner that evening Georgina accelerated her
uncle's pleasure by asking him to arrange for a
telegram to be sent to Wally informing him of her
decision to stay in Ireland for at least a week. She
felt rather disturbed by the thought of what Wally's
feelings would be when he received it. Their work
in northern England was almost completed, only
her signature was needed on the final papers, but
she consoled herself with the thought that she really
did need a break and that a few days here or there
would make very little difference to the success of
the venture. She did not instruct that a forwarding
address should be included in the message and she
was guiltily aware that this, too, would annoy him
intensely, but she was reluctant to have him haring
across to Ireland to join her. She needed complete
freedom to cope with the downfall of Lian Ardulian
and Wally's presence might distract her from her
objective; an objective which was fast reaching the
proportions of an obsession.

She was certain now that her weighing up of the
situation had been a correct one. Lian's manner,
during the afternoon while he had shown her
around the grounds, had run true to form: exactly
as she had calculated it would. His eyes had never
seemed to leave her face while he entertained her
with numerous amusing anecdotes concerning the

doings of some of his tenants and, in spite of the knowledge that he was being flatteringly attentive for a purpose, she had been unable to subdue her amusement at his deliberate exaggeration of funny situations that had arisen when strangers had come up against the illogical reasoning of the local characters. Even now, as she recalled to mind an incident he had recounted, she had to quell a threatened surge of laughter. Unbelievingly, she had listened while he had told her, poker-faced, about an American tourist who had been driving along, enjoying the peace of the countryside, when he was suddenly confused to find his way blocked by a gate over one half of a level crossing. He had waited, undecided, to see if the other half of the gate would swing across, indicating the arrival of a train, or if the obstructing half would swing back to allow him to proceed— but nothing happened. Finally, sick of waiting, he had stuck his thumb on his horn and and let it blare away until Paddy Murphy appeared from out of his signal box. 'Say, fella,' he had shouted as Paddy ambled towards him, 'what's the cause of the delay?'

Paddy had scratched his head. 'Delay? What delay?'

The American had been almost apoplectic. 'The gates, man, the gates!' he had shouted, nodding vigorously in the direction of the offending obstacle. 'Why are they only half open?'

Paddy's eyes had lit up with slow understanding. 'Oh, them!' he looked his contempt of the American's ignorance. 'Why, to be sure, I was half expecting a train!'

Georgina felt extremely foolish when a loud

chuckle from her uncle brought her back to the realization that she was staring at her plate with a large vacant grin.

'What thoughts are amusing you, alannah?' her uncle teased, his expansive smile showing the extent of his satisfaction. She coloured swiftly and looked towards Lian at the head of the table, but the look was averted when she saw amusement dancing in his eyes. What a fool she must look in their sight, a vulnerable fool with a head easily turned by a silvered tongue! Mentally, she groped for and found the hard core of anger that sustained her in moments of weakening and its presence allowed her to smile captivatingly at them both.

'I was mentally recapping on a wonderful day, Uncle,' she lied lightly. She pretended not to notice the quick look of triumph Michael sent across the table to Lian which, although she did not look at the recipient, she felt sure was returned. A sudden wave of dejection swept over her, leaving her deadly tired. Her fatigue must have shown itself in the peaked whiteness of her face, because Lian rose quickly from his seat to bend over her.

'Don't you feel well, Gina?' he asked sharply, his deep blue eyes searching her wan face. His expression of concern seemed almost genuine, but she was too depressed to care. Sleep and solitude beckoned invitingly, so that it was all she could do to whisper: 'If you'll excuse me, it's been a long day, I'd like to go upstairs.'

Softly Lian cursed himself for a fool. 'Of course you must go to your room, I should have remembered earlier that you're still an invalid who needs

46

plenty of rest, but, selfishly, I put my own pleasure in your company before your welfare. Come,' to her consternation she felt herself scooped up into his arms, 'I'll take you to your room and call Kate to help you into bed.'

Ignoring her protest that she could quite easily walk, he carried her effortlessly across the dimly lighted hall, up the shallow stairs, and along the passageway to her room. He did not release her until he reached her bedside and even after lowering her did not immediately straighten, but remained to lean over her with a fathomless expression on his dark face. He was close, suffocatingly close, but she could not escape because his arms imprisoned her on either side. She turned her head away to avoid his look which was even more disturbing than physical contact had been, and blamed the flood of weakness that set her body trembling on the illness she had not yet recovered from. She did not stop to ask herself why she found his seriousness so disconcerting; why the defences that held so firmly against his deliberate charm should threaten to crumble when that charm was not in evidence. Tears she could not contain flooded her eyes, bringing from him a rough exclamation of dismay. The gentle touch of his hand as he turned her face towards him forced from her a soundless gasp of distress and to her horror her mouth began to quiver uncontrollably.

'Hush, mavourneen,' his soft voice attempted to soothe, 'why are you so upset, don't you feel well?'

When she did not answer, his startling eyes darkened with anxiety and he straightened and strode across to a bell which he pressed long and hard, presumably to summon Kate. By the time he returned to her side she had her weakness tightly under control. Her closed eyelids screened him from sight, but she could sense his nearness in the taut silence that filled the room. Although he did not speak again, she could feel his searching eyes probing her face for unendurable seconds and the effort to remain calm took so much out of her that Kate's hurried appearance was an indescribable relief. He spoke a few terse words to the old woman before striding from the room, leaving behind him such an aura of anti-climax Georgina was unable to cope. Distressed beyond reason, she threw herself into Kate's comforting arms and wept until she fell into an exhausted sleep.

The next morning she was furious with herself when she recalled, with burning cheeks, her parlous state of the previous night. Refreshing sleep had rid her of the physical weakness upon which she readily heaped the blame for the vacillating emotions which had made her so vulnerable to the power Lian Ardulian wielded under his screening cloak of easy charm. If any warning of his power were needed, she should have found it yesterday, as she had wandered through the picture gallery studying a dozen or more family portraits of previous Chiefs of the Name. They had looked swashbuckling rebels, all of them, with black rogue eyebrows cocked knavishly above blue eyes alight with humour; proud, flaring nostrils, and mouths that promised to bestow a storm of kisses upon a captured wench or a taunting tirade of impudent abuse upon a foe. All of them had been painted leaning negligently against the same wide ledge of stone above a fireplace that had chipped deep into its stone the family emblem: an eagle with wings outstretched ready for flight and underneath it the motto: We Dare All!

Even allowing for the casual informality of the riding kit Lian had elected to wear for his sittings, and for the twentieth-century artist who had painted him, the same rebel pride that had urged on his wild ancestors to pillage and plunder their way across the breadth of Ireland to their west coast eyrie was there in his portrait for all who had eyes to see. We dare all! The first chief had dared all to seize the prize that was Eagles' Mount. To what lengths was the present chief prepared to go to retain it?

She shivered and slipped out of bed to move across to the window towards the view which drew her with a strange compulsion. Lian Ardulian, she admitted, had an extra weapon in his armoury, one which previous members of his line would have found useless in an era of primitive simplicity but one which, in the present sophisticated society, he would find invaluable: deviousness. One would never be able to tell for certain which course he intended to follow, so Georgina knew that her best weapon of defence would be the ice-cool, needle-sharp brain she used to such advantage in business. It must never be allowed to let her down. How would she fare, for instance, if instead of playing the restrained charmer, which had been his role until now, he should revert to type and allow rein to the passions she knew lurked shallow under the surface of his amiability? A wild thrill of fear coursed through her veins at the thought and her eyes, grey as peat smoke, widened with apprehension. As she worried about the disturbing possibility, she betrayed her agitation by plucking nervously at the great drapes that framed the window. Thank goodness her head was clear again; except for the worrying lapses which now occurred only when she grew tired, she was almost back to normal. If she remembered to avoid his presence whenever she felt fatigued there should not be the remotest possibility of a repeat of last night's disastrous performance.

After breakfast, and after being assured that she felt completely well, Lian proposed that she should accompany him on a visit to one of his tenants. She agreed with an alacrity not entirely assumed for his benefit, and hurried upstairs to her room to fetch a coat while he strode off to arrange transport. She was not prepared, upon stepping outside a few minutes later, for the sight of him driving up to the front of the house in a painted jaunting cart with a high-stepping mare frisking between its shafts, and surprise kept her silent until he jumped down beside her and prepared to assist her on to it.

A gurgle of laughter escaped her when he lifted her on to the cart and she felt an unfamiliar swaying sensation as she sat sideways, her feet resting on a narrow wooden ledge. The mare whinneyed and took a dainty step forward, as if aware and resentful of her amusement, and Georgina gave a cry and clutched nervously at the side of the cart when the sudden movement almost unbalanced her.

Lian gave a deep-throated chuckle. 'There's no need to be nervous,' he assured her. 'Sheena here is a more reliable form of transport than one of your sleek American automobiles, and a sight less temperamental, I'll warrant.' He swung himself up into the driver's bench and patted the empty space beside him. 'Would you prefer to sit here, up front, or do you feel safer where you are?' he queried. The ambiguous words were accompanied by a challenging glint which Georgina felt it politic to ignore, but colour rose in her cheeks when after she had answered him primly, 'I'm quite comfortable here, thank you,' he threw back his dark head and laughed aloud before tightening the reins and encouraging Sheena with a clicking noise that the mare quickly interpreted as a signal to move off.

She relaxed in her seat and shrugged off her coat; it was a mild, calm morning and already the sun held a promise of heat. She began to enjoy the pleasant sensation of being rocked and swayed behind the fleet-footed mare, and her first real sight of the country outside of the boundaries of Eagles' Mount was breathtaking. They were still high up, but were descending gradually towards the lush green valley that cradled in its bosom the opalescent lake she had seen from her window. Behind her, the fortress they had just left seemed to cling with an eagle's tenacity to the black mountain that had spawned it and not even the sun's casting rays could gild the sombre mass with any form of beauty. She turned her head away from its fearful majesty to feast her eyes upon the gentle beauty of the inland slopes. It was so quiet, only the rhythmic clip-clop of Sheena's hooves against the hard path disturbed the heavy silence and not even a smoke curl from a cabin chimney disturbed the still air. When they reached the bottom of the mountain she felt she was in an enormous amphitheatre with mountains piled on mountains, covered with heath and heather. In the sheltered valley, protected from Atlantic gales by the great shoulders of rock, lush woodlands contrasted darkly green against the lighter-shaded peat bogs.

Lian, after a couple of backward glances, seemed content to let the scenery speak for itself, and she was grateful for his understanding. After a lifetime spent among New York's hard concrete and garish illuminations, she was not geared to the unexpected beauty that had fallen so suddenly into her lap; she needed time to assimilate it—to grapple with the spell it was weaving around her. Lian was acute enough to perceive this, and it was not until they had travelled for about an hour that he intruded into her absorption, and only then because he caught sight of his tenant, Daniel Kavanagh, bent low over two sticks as he carried on his back a heavy basket full of peat from the bog to his cottage which could just be seen in the distance.

'Good morning to you, Daniel!' Lian hailed him as he drew in the reins.

Georgina looked up and saw a man, once tall but now stooped with age, his withered face split into a smile that left them in no doubt of their welcome. He slid the heavy load from his back and even while he straightened he reached out to clasp Lian's hand between his own.

'Sure, and it's pleased I am to see you this day, Ardulian, with Deirdre back home this minute. Yes, my daughter's back home just now!' This was said with such fierce pride it brought a lump to

Georgina's throat. Whoever this frail old man was, there was no doubting his devotion to his daughter, Deirdre. Her name, when voiced with such breathless excitement, sounded like a soft endearment.

Lian gave a sharp exclamation of pleasure. 'Deirdre home? That's wonderful news, I can't wait to see her again. Quickly, Daniel, get your load into the car and we'll give her a surprise by turning up together!'

Nothing loath, the old man clambered on to the car and Lian made a swift introduction before setting off.

'Daniel, this is Gina Rooney, niece of our old friend Michael, and one of our American cousins.' Then, to Georgina, 'Meet Daniel Kavanagh, father of the sweetest girl in Ireland!'

She quickly suppressed the pang which for some unexplainable reason these words produced and acknowledged the old man's shy nod with a quick smile. In a brogue so thick it reminded her forcibly that she was in the heart of the Gaeltacht, the region where ancient Irish speech and customs are still preserved and where English is still a second language, he managed to convey to her his pleasure in making her acquaintance, and as they jogged along in the direction of his home, he stumbled haltingly through a conversation of which Georgina understood less than half but which, as it was liberally sprinkled with the name Deirdre, she guessed was mainly concerned with his daughter and his joy at her homecoming. She felt a surge of anger against the unknown Deirdre. Obviously, her visits were a rare and wonderful occurrence in his life, and

Georgina, who still felt the loss of her own father, wondered how anyone could be so heartless as to neglect such an aged parent. The sweetest girl in Ireland, Lian had called her, which indicated that he, too, was enamoured by the girl. Somehow, Georgina felt, she was not going to be drawn under the spell of the paragon she was about to meet.

Ten minutes later she had her first sight of the girl in all their thoughts. As Daniel's cottage gradually came into view—first a curl of smoke from the stubby chimney that topped the thatched roof, then whitewashed walls smothered in ivy and rambling briar roses in first bud—she could just make out the figure of a girl half stretched out along the top of the low stone wall that surrounded the fertile strip of land around the cottage. Even from a distance she compelled attention. The poise of her head on her well-shaped neck, and the unconsciously provocative emphasis laid on her curves by the clinging peasant blouse she wore were noticeable enough, but when they drew near enough to attract her attention and she jumped eagerly from the wall and began to run towards them, Georgina saw that she was one of the loveliest girls she had ever seen. Free as a bird, she flew in their direction, her long red hair, fired by sunlight, streaming out behind her and her eyes sparkling green as the dew-laden grass she crushed beneath her naked feet as she ran. She looked like a film star playing the part of an Irish colleen, and if a camera boom had suddenly appeared above her head and a film director had shouted 'cut' Georgina would not have been surprised, because although Deirdre was a child of Erin with her roots dug deep in Irish soil, it was obvious that the cloak of poverty and deprivation had not been allowed to sit for long on her smooth shoulders.

Lian checked the mare, and even before the car wheels had stopped turning he jumped down to stand with arms outstretched to receive the speeding girl. Seconds later she was in his arms, laughing, hugging, and kissing him as if too long deprived of his company, and being hugged and kissed in return. Georgina felt an intruder as she and the smiling Daniel watched their enthusiastic meeting; Daniel was entitled to watch, he was one of them, but she felt shut out, an outsider somehow caught up in the middle of a family reunion. But she managed to hide her chagrin and to smile a greeting when Lian finally remembered her existence and indicated her presence to the excited girl.

'Deirdre, I'd like you to meet Georgina Rooney, a young Irish-American who's staying with us while she recuperates from a recent illness. I hope you two will be friends; you could give a lot to each other.'

He had no chance to elaborate upon his ambiguous statement, because Deirdre immediately turned all her attention upon Georgina as well as all of her considerable charm. With wide eyes distended, she quickly moved over to Georgina and extended her hand in an impulsive gesture of friendship. 'I'm delighted to meet you, Georgina,' she spoke with obvious sincerity. 'I hope you don't mind being called Georgina on first acquaintance?'

'Of course not,' Georgina replied, her suspicions submerged by the friendly approach of the candid-eyed girl who looked as if she should be doing anything other than running wild in the depths of the Gaeltacht.

'And you'll call me Deirdre?' she asked beguilingly.

'Yes, please,' Georgina answered without hesitation, quite won over by her warm sincerity.

Laughing and chattering they all piled back on to the cart for the few minutes' journey to the house. Deirdre sat up front, next to Lian, but talked excitedly over her shoulder to Georgina as the mare ambled along.

'You must come into the cottage for a meal, Georgina. Lian and Father have something very important to discuss, but I'll want all the help I can get to persuade this stubborn old man that the request Lian and I have plotted in our letters to make of him is granted.' A cold hand squeezed Georgina's heart, but she took herself sternly to task. It was no business of hers if Lian and Deirdre corresponded regularly. As for the request that needed Daniel's sanction, that, too, was none of her business.

When they reached the cottage, Deirdre, without a trace of misgiving, ushered her through the doorway into a room so impoverished it could have been described as primitive. Daniel moved immediately towards the pile of dried peat stacked beside the open-hearthed fireplace and lifted a couple more pieces to top the ones already smouldering under a large smoke-blackened kettle that hung from a hook and chain above the fire. Then, while Deirdre lifted crockery from a shabby dresser and began placing it around a scrubbed wooden table, he drew forward one of the four chairs that were ranged along the wall and placed it near to the fire for Georgina: She forced herself not to betray the pity her surroundings aroused and kept her eyes from straying lest her curiosity should cause her hostess embarrassment. But she need not have worried. When Lian casually drew up a chair for himself next to Daniel and began talking in an earnest undertone to the old man, Deirdre's face took on an expression of pleased anticipation and her feet—now clad in soft-soled shoes—fairly danced over the stone-paved floor as she prepared the meal for her guests.

The kettle was just beginning to sing and everything was ready, when Deirdre elevated an eyebrow in Georgina's direction and silently mimed to her to come outside until Lian and Daniel had finished their talk. Without disturbing the engrossed men, they moved outside into the garden and made by silent consent towards the chicken run that took up most of the space at the back of the house.

Deirdre could hardly contain her impatience. 'I do hope Lian manages to talk him round,' she stressed, her face showing worry for the first time.

'So do I,' Georgina answered slowly, 'if it means so much to you.'

'Means so much ...!' Deirdre looked shocked. 'Oh, I forgot, you have no idea what they're discussing! I'm sorry, Georgina, you must think me a complete idiot nattering away as if we were involved in a deep, dark secret, but the subject of the talk is so important to me that I simply can't bear to mention it in case anything should go wrong. Silly of me, isn't it, but I've a superstitious feeling that if I should discuss it too much everything will fall through.'

Georgina understood the garbled message. When a girl and a man were as attached as she and Lian, it stood to reason they should not want their innermost feeling exposed to prying eyes and idle discussion. She felt a sudden pity for the girl she felt sure was waiting to hear that her father had given his permission for her marriage to Lian Ardulian. Perhaps Daniel, friendly though he was towards his chief, was hesitant to give his daughter into his keeping. Did he realize, as Deirdre obviously did not, what an unscrupulous man he was? Should she reveal that only yesterday Lian Ardulian had been scheming with her uncle to flirt with herself in order to further his own ends? As she inwardly urged herself to tell Deirdre the facts, the door opened and Lian stood smiling triumphantly at Deirdre.

'Lian, is it all right? Have you managed to persuade him?' Deirdre waited with agonizing uncertainty for his answer, and when his smile broadened and he nodded an affirmative, she gave a squeal of delight and rushed into his waiting arms.

It was too late. Georgina told herself that the pain she felt was for Deirdre—compassion for a girl oblivious to the flaws possessed by the man she loved. One thing was certain; she could not speak now. Deirdre would have to discover for herself the shortcomings of the man she planned to marry.

# CHAPTER FIVE

GEORGINA was most surprised when, after Deirdre's excitement had died down, Lian prepared to leave the Kavanaghs. He excused them both from sharing the meal Deirdre had prepared by stating firmly that he had other pressing matters to attend to. Deirdre was disappointed, but not dismayed, and Georgina wondered how she could bear to allow her new fiancé to depart so suddenly without even a swift discussion about future plans. She searched for some sign of hurt when she made her goodbyes, but Deirdre's candid face still displayed the unreserved joy it had shown earlier. Reluctantly, Georgina followed Lian to the jaunting cart, but as she waved her farewells to the Kavanaghs her brow was wrinkled with puzzlement and a dozen unasked questions trembled on her lips.

When the two figures had faded from sight, she sighed and relaxed once more in her seat. Lian seemed well pleased with himself. She stole a glance at his firmly etched profile and saw a smile of satisfaction curl his lips. He startled her by asking, 'What did you think of Deirdre, do you think you two will become friends?'

She was confused into stammering, 'How . . . how can I tell on such short acquaintance?'

His eyebrows shot up and he answered dryly: 'With some people one knows instinctively as soon as one meets them,' he hesitated for the space of half a breath, then continued, 'as I did when I first met you.'

Anger kept her tongue-tied for a second and before she could find words to indict him, he carried on speaking as if his cool lie had not been voiced. 'Deirdre is a wonderful girl. Her mother died when she was just fourteen and she almost broke her heart when Daniel insisted upon keeping a promise he had made to his wife by sending her to London to live with her aunt, her mother's sister, until she had finished her education. She resisted Daniel's wish with everything that was in her, but Daniel knew she had a fine brain that was wasting away through lack of suitable tuition. Anyway, when Miss Docherty, the schoolmistress, added her pressure to Daniel's, Deirdre had to give in. She finished her schooling in London, then afterwards she went to the Royal Academy of Dramatic Art which, at that time, was her Mecca; her ultimate ambition, and there she exceeded even our wildest hopes.' He glanced around to make sure he was not boring her and when he saw her rapt expression, carried on. 'She is now a successful actress and very much in demand, but in every contract she signs she insists upon a clause being inserted to the effect that for three months in each year she is free of all obligation to the theatre. Those three months,' he finished simply, 'are Daniel's. Perhaps now you can understand the old man's pride when he says: "My daughter's back home just now".'

A lump lodged in Georgina's throat and she had to blink rapidly to disperse the tears the simple tale had culled up. But Lian sensed her distress and his voice harshened as he told her, 'Don't cry just for Deirdre and Daniel—cry for all the families in Kerry! In every village, in every cottage, and even isolated hamlets stuck up on mountainsides, there are aged parents living alone, wondering if the Lord will be good enough to let them see their sons and daughters just once more before they die. Like birds migrating from the nest, they've flown to every part of the globe. There are priests in Chicago; bridge-builders in South America; road-diggers in England; even our girls are nursing in hospitals scattered all over the globe and the young ones that are left are itching to join them. Do you wonder,' his voice grated so harshly she jumped, 'that I would think no sacrifice too great if it achieved the righting of such a wrong!'

Hypnotized by the force of his feelings, she stared into his eyes, now ice-blue and glittering coldly. His fury was so intense that she withdrew from it with a gasp of dismay, and the sound seemed to bring him to his senses. His change of mood was so swift she was left gasping, one moment he was glowering down at her as if she alone were responsible for the desertion of Ireland's children and the next he had thrown back his head and was laughing aloud, his mercurial temperament soaring from rage to amusement in a matter of seconds.

Twinkling down into her shocked face, he apologized, 'I'm sorry if my diabolical mood upset you, Gina, please forgive me. I'm afraid that when I get on to that subject I'm apt to give full rein to my temper, and I forgot you're not used to such displays of feeling.' Two spears of blue suddenly trained themselves upon her flushed face and his mouth twisted into a wry smile. 'How wonderful it must be never to allow emotion to intrude upon common sense! To be able to think dispassionately on every subject without ever having to consider the question of human rights and old loyalties.' She felt herself accused and instinctively made to answer, but he forestalled her. 'But enough of that,' he gave the ambling mare a flick with the reins so that she might pick up speed, 'I've talked too much of politics. I brought you out here to enjoy yourself and I intend to see that you do.'

He turned his back upon her when Sheena picked up speed and she sank limply back in her seat, only then aware that her hands were clenched tightly and her body taut with fear. She felt exhausted by the buffeting his words had given her and seared by the contemptuous innuendos that had flown from his tongue. How dared he accuse her of being heartless and uncaring of human problems? She *did* care about Deirdre and Daniel and all the others too, but she simply had not known that such tragic circumstances existed or she would certainly have built the factory in Ireland.

She pulled up short, the reminder of the factory acting like a cold douche on her seething brain. How diabolically clever he was! Ice-water ran through her veins, cooling her feelings and bringing sanity in its wake. She had actually begun to believe that the prime factor behind his impassioned words was the welfare of his tenants; just one more twist to her heartstrings and she would have been promising him anything! Appalled by her narrow escape, she sank back, deep in thought, and proceeded to marshall her resources, grimly resolving that Lian Ardulian would not find her so susceptible to his next onslaught.

It soon became evident why he had chosen to bring Sheena on the expedition; no other form of transport could have negotiated the route they travelled half so well as the sturdy little mare. They left the luxuriant valley scenery behind them and began to ascend an uneven, winding path edged with boulders that might easily have been strewn there by a giant's hand. Each sharp, unexpected bend brought into focus a different aspect of the beauty around them, and she paid rapt attention as fragments of blue lake and mauve-shrouded peaks were displayed for a tantalizing few seconds before being whisked away from sight behind outcrops of grey rock. They covered miles of streams, tarns, and magnificent cliff scenery before Lian pulled up on a narrow stone bridge, its sides so thickly covered with greenery that one could imagine it had grown there, to allow her to digest the sight of rushing water cascading down the mountainside, tumbling over the craggy face in a silver stream until it disappeared with gurgling insistence under the bridge beneath their feet.

'It's beautiful, simply beautiful!' she breathed.

Lian smiled. 'This is the Gap of Dunloe which, legend has it, the great Finn McCoul himself formed with one blow of his mighty sword, but,' he teased suddenly, 'you don't have to believe that unless you want to.'

But she could believe anything might have happened in a region so steeped in lore, where leprechauns and 'little people' were spoken of with bated breath and bites of food and sips of milk were still left out last thing at night for 'them'. Kate had volubly assured her that it was most dangerous to upset 'them' and had become quite huffy when Georgina had scornfully laughed away her superstitious beliefs, but now, as she deliberated, she was not so sure—there was magic in the air, she could almost feel it.

'Are you hungry?' Lian's mundane question broke the spell. When she admitted that she was, he jumped from the cart, pulled a wicker basket from under his seat, and held out a hand to assist her down. 'Come on, then, let's find a comfortable bit of grass where we can share out whatever Kate has packed in here for us.' They picked a spot a few yards upstream where shady bushes overhung crystal-clear pools and the water set a myriad rainbow-hued splashes dancing in the sunlight as it washed over large boulders obstructing its course. On a saucer of springy turf he spread out a rug and when she sat down he opened the basket with the air of a man ready to do justice to whatever he found inside.

There was ham wedged thickly between freshly baked rolls; delicious little pasties of flaky pastry filled with a savoury mixture of minced beef and finely diced vegetables, and for dessert crisp green apples that crunched satisfyingly between their teeth when they bit into them. Georgina could not remember ever having enjoyed a meal more. When her apple had been neatly demolished, she threw away the core and lay back, replete, to bask in the ever-increasing warmth of the sun. With closed eyes she listened to the shrill warbling of an unseen bird as it flew from branch to branch calling its mate. She felt a movement and knew that Lian had followed her example and was stretched out beside her less than an arm's length away, but she did not open her eyes. She was aware of the noise of the stream, exaggerated in the still air, then imperceptibly the noise grew quieter until finally it faded altogether, and she slept.

She had no idea for how long. She woke fretfully, sensing an irritating tickle against her face, and lifted her hand to brush away what she thought was an offending fly. But her eyes flew open when her wrist was captured in a firm grip and her breath caught in quick surprise when Lian's dark head obscured the sky. As he leant across, smiling tormentingly, she saw that he was holding a long piece of grass which he had obviously just used to tickle her awake. Colour flooded her cheeks and she struggled to sit upright, but he leant closer, not touching, but his intimidating nearness causing her to sink back, grappling with emotions of confused anger.

The sky above was no bluer than the eyes that twinkled down at her, but their message culled up no answering warmth from her bleak heart. His siege had begun; not even his newly engaged state was to deter him from carrying out the plan evolved by her uncle. A shudder of revulsion ran through her; she felt humiliated at the idea of being used in such a way. But although she would have to suffer his spurious attentions in order to allay his suspicions, her revenge when it came would be sweet. She wondered dully if strength of mind could overcome physical frailty; whether a mind, however strictly controlled, could contain the traitorous impulses of a weak body, and on the heels of the thought came the challenge that was to put her to the test.

He was a master of non-verbal communication. Silently, he made his first tentative sortie by stroking his fingers gently down her arm with a slow caressing movement that sent shivers down her spine. Blue eyes locked with grey and the message she received told her: *I'm interested in you. I'm attracted and I mean to know why!* It filled her with a mixture of hate, desire and fear. A smile curved his lips and the exploratory fingers slid beyond her wrist to clasp her cold hand in his. This was the point of no return. She knew enough of the game of love to realize that now was the moment either to rebuff or encourage; if she were to show annoyance or dismay he would release her immediately, probably to try again another day.

Gently she squeezed his hand in return.

For an infinitesimal second she glimpsed—was it disappointment?—in his dark-lashed eyes, but then every thought was blocked out when he lowered his lips and captured her trembling mouth in a kiss that told her most effectively: *I am a man and I want you desperately!*

Her first instinctive reaction to his deceit was to scream her aversion of it, but just before she lost control her cool brain took over and ordered her back to the fray. So, slowly at first, she responded. As she allowed her lips to move under his, his grasp tightened and he forced her backward until she felt the ground hard beneath her shoulders. When he raised his head and whispered 'Gina!' a wild surge of triumph thrilled her. Incredibly, the eagle had been hooded!

More confidently, she raised her hand and stroked the lean planes of his cheek with a feather-light touch that inflamed him further. His eyes were liquid, molten blue flame, no longer merely curious but filled with a mixture of masculine aggressiveness allied with wonder. She had succeeded completely in turning the tables on the Eagle of Ardulian, but even as she tried to savour the triumph such an achievement warranted an ache filled her heart with such pain she flinched visibly and turned her face away when he would have kissed her again.

He laughed shortly and released her, to begin searching his pockets for cigarettes. She watched him as he lighted one, narrowing his eyes against the flare of the match, and noted with satisfaction that his hand was trembling and that he inhaled deeply as if in need of an aid to self-control. She hated him, not only for his deliberately planned advances, but because of his disloyalty to Deirdre. She felt desperately sorry for the girl betrothed to a man who might, in his own way, return her love but who had admitted that he would think no sacrifice too great to gain his own ends.

He threw away his cigarette and turned once more to look at her. She felt impaled by his hard blue stare as it travelled the length of her and finally came to rest on her mobile mouth. She forced a smile, but his brooding face did not respond. She was puzzled by his silence, his air of disquiet, and decided to shock him into speech.

Stretching lazily, she gave a yawn and pouted: 'What's wrong, Lian? I was just beginning to enjoy our ... togetherness? Surely you're not allowing thoughts of Deirdre to intrude upon our efforts to get to know one another better?' She laughed, a bitter mocking laugh that somehow managed to sound teasing, and moved slightly so that her slim thigh brushed against his.

'Deirdre?' His voice grated. 'What has Deirdre to do with us?'

She sat up to brush away dried grass from her shoulder, giving the action all of her attention. 'I had the impression you two were very much attracted to each other, but perhaps I'm wrong?'

'No,' he deliberated, watching her through eyes narowed into slits, 'you're not wrong. Not, at least, on that score.'

Her eyebrows swept up, questioning his ambiguity, but the light words she had meant to utter dried in her throat when she sensed the danger in his tensely held body. His eagle profile was grim, he seemed poised on the brink of violence, his curbed feelings held taut on a leash stretched to the uttermost. Only then did she become fully aware of how dangerous was the game she had elected to play. Panic stirred the serenity of her grey eyes which up until then had managed to mirror cool discipline, and the blunder did not escape his notice. His grim smile of satisfaction accelerated her fear, causing her to jump up in an effort to evade the fierce emotion she knew was about to erupt; but her move was made too late. Even as she rose, he sprang to his feet and caught her by the waist in a grip of of steel.

'You dare to play games,' he gritted through clenched teeth, 'so you must suffer the consequences!'

Desperately she struggled, certain now that he was way past the stage of gentle flirtation and angry with herself for allowing her foolishness and lack of experience to lead her into such a trap. As his head swooped down she found her voice and his seeking lips were a mere breath away when she uttered:

'Lian, I'm not playing games. I love you!'

He halted immediately, his warm breath fanning her cheek, and warily searched her guileless face. She withstood his look without a tremble, but her heartbeat only returned to normal when she saw his wild passion fade into gentleness. The sweetness of his smile and the dawning wonder of his expression was an actor's masterpiece.

'Can it be true?' The Eagle of Ardulian seemed dazed with doubt.

She swallowed her shame and whispered ardently, 'Very true, darling Lian. On the first night I arrived at Eagles' Mount I fell in love with a charming voice and with a strong pair of arms which when they enfolded me seemed to convince me that at last I'd come home. Please tell me you love me, too, my darling, because I can't bear to think of how I'll live without you if you say otherwise!'

His tone betrayed none of the triumph he must have been feeling when he folded her against his heart and breathed against her throat, 'Gina, mavourneen, my love, I can hardly believe the wonderful things you're saying! That night when I lifted you into my arms and looked down at your pale little face, so full of strain but yet so beautiful, I knew that at last I had found the woman I had waited all my life for. I wanted, there and then, to shout it to the world, but I had to contain my soul in patience and wait for our relationship to take its course. You see,' he prised her face from his shoulder and looked down at her with a frown of puzzlement, 'I'd had a totally erroneous impression of you from your uncle. I had expected to find you very cool and sophisticated, a dedicated businesswoman with no warmth or depth, and instead I found you sweet and understanding, fun-loving, and adorably feminine. Believe me, I'll have some hard words to say to that old scoundrel Rooney, about his blind stupidity!'

'Oh, Lian!' She choked out a laugh and hoped he would take the tears that were chasing down her cheeks for tears of joy. She could not explain even to herself why she was crying or why, when everything was going as she had planned, her heart should feel so heavy its presence was an agonizing ache. He dried her tears, his eagle profile softened with a tenderness he seemed to don at will, then he picked her up in his arms. He carried her across to the jaunting cart and placed her in the seat next to his.

'No more weeping, Gina, mavourneen,' he laughingly commanded as he wiped away the last glistening tear, 'or Kate will never believe that you come of your own free will to be the future mistress of Eagles' Mount.'

Then his mouth descended, and her gasp of dismay was smothered by a kiss that threatened the complete annihilation of all her future plans.

# CHAPTER SIX

WHEN they arrived back at Eagles' Mount Lian
swept into the great hall and yelled loudly until
Michael and Kate made their hurried appearance;
they stood open-mouthed, watching, as he waltzed
Georgina around the floor like a man possessed. His
exultant face and Georgina's flustered embarrassment must have given them a hint of what to expect,
because they both began to bombard him with
excited questions.

'Glory be!' Kate raised her hands in supplication
as curiosity overwhelmed her. 'Won't you tell a
body what's going on?'

Michael's eyes sparkled with anticipation when
he pleaded. 'Put the girl down, won't you, Lian, and
tell us what's pleasing you so much you feel the
need to dance. Is it a pot of gold you've found?'

Lian gave her a last rapid twirl before stopping
with such abruptness she had to hang on to his arm
while she waited for the room to cease its wild gyra-
tions. He pressed her closer to his side and laughed
down into her scarlet face before answering.

'Better than that, Michael, I've found a lasting
treasure! Congratulate me, both of you, I'm the
luckiest man in the world today.' He pushed her
forward, grinning widely at her confusion, and presented her: 'Meet the future mistress of Eagles'
Mount!'

Kate gave a delighted squeal and flung her arms around Georgina's neck. 'Heaven be praised!' she cried, 'This is a happy day for all of us.'

Michael seemed to have lost all power of speech. He stared at Lian as if he could hardly believe his ears, then finally turned his mute look upon Georgina as if urging her either to confirm or to deny. She could not meet his eyes. Treacherous though she knew him—knew them both—to be, her own actions shamed her so much that she felt degraded. But to Michael, her downcast eyes and flushed cheeks spelled out a shyness which amply confirmed Lian's incredible statement. Georgina was astonished to see her uncle's eyes fill with tears and to hear his voice tremble with feeling when he reached out to clasp her hands in his.

'Georgina, love, you've picked a fine man, the best in all Ireland, I couldn't have chosen better for you myself. I wish you happiness, of course, but I've no real need to, I know you'll have it in ample measure. Bless you, darling, you've made me a very happy man this day.' Georgina could stand no more. As she looked around at their smiling faces she knew she had to escape, if only for a few short minutes, from the web of deceit she had helped to weave. She backed away with a trapped, hunted look, then fled up the staircase to her room.

Once there, she paced the floor in a fever of doubt, wondering just how far Lian Ardulian was prepared to go. She had expected a light flirtation, something he might manage, given luck, to keep from Deirdre, but his exuberance, his determination to proclaim to the world their supposed alliance had her confused and worried. What was his intention? Surely, her heart almost skipped a beat, he was not prepared to carry out his spoken intention of marrying her even if in the process it meant breaking Deirdre's heart? Not even he could be so utterly callous!

A knock at her door made her tense, but she relaxed when Kate bustled in, smiling broadly. 'I've come to help you get over your little bit of nerves, my dear,' she comforted. 'To be sure, you've no need to let the idea of marrying Himself overwhelm you. Great man though he is, at the bottom of him he's just like any other—lonely and a bit desolate without a wife to share his troubles. But that's all ended now, praise be, and his dear mother would be happy this day if she knew her boy had found happiness at last.'

Georgina mustered a nervous smile. 'His mother ...?' she questioned, edging Kate into supplying more information.

'Dead this five years past, God rest her soul.' Kate crossed herself fervently. 'And his father two years before that. Yes, it's a lonely life the boy's had since they both departed this world and not even by driving himself into the ground with work has he managed to fill the gap they left behind them.' She wiped a tear from the corner of her eye, then went on brightly: 'But all that's over now. I speak on behalf of all in Kerry when I say that hearts will rejoice this day and glasses will be lifted high in toasts to the Chief and to the bride we know will bring him the happiness he so well deserves.' This last sentiment was spoken in a voice so weighted with tears Georgina winced. She hardly dared to think of the hurt she would inflict upon the Chief's people when she denounced him as an unprincipled rogue, but, for the sake of any future victims, it would have to be done—and soon.

That evening, Lian insisted they must all dress for dinner, which was to be a special celebration meal for just the three of them. Kate had promised to do justice to the occasion by cooking something extra special; candles were to be lighted in the enormous silver candelabra that had last seen service when Lian's mother had presided over the dinner-table, and silver plate and crystal goblets were to be unearthed for the first time in years. Georgina, her head awhirl with the swiftness with which events were overtaking her, searched her wardrobe for something to wear for the occasion. Only one dress presented itself as even remotely suitable; a cocktail sheath of white taffeta shot through with silver threads, its scooped-out neckline and armbands trimmed with strips of heavy silver embroidery. Why her uncle had included it in her luggage she did not know, but she was grateful for the happy chance that had guided his hand.

As she began to get ready, she was filled with a mounting feeling of exhilaration, a feeling which prompted her to take special care with her appearance. She gave detailed attention to her make-up, shadowing her grey eyes carefully so that they reflected the blueness of a summer lake overhung by haze, then she brushed her long hair smooth and arranged it loosely so that its black velvet softness nestled against the creamy whiteness of her shoul-

75

ders. Lipstick was hardly necessary, her mouth had blushed fiery red since Lian's tempestuous kisses and was even now burning under the touch of her fingers, so she traced a mere film of pearly pink against its warmth.

She slipped on the dress—one Stella had bought for her recently but which she had never before worn—and took stock of her appearance in the full-length mirror attached to her wardrobe. Outlined against the massive pieces of furniture, her figure seemed to lack substance. She looked so ethereal she might, she fancied, have been a ghost from bygone days—the wife, perhaps, of one of the earlier Ardulians whose spirit was drawn back to the fortress that had witnessed such scenes of passion as those eagle-affined men might have aroused. Her wraith-slim figure melted into the heavy gloom of the dusk-shaded room, retreating from the sight of her own starry-eyed confusion, and she hesitated at the door to compose her wayward thoughts before answering the gong that told her dinner was almost ready.

Lian was waiting at the bottom of the stairs; a very different Lian from the one who up until then had dressed in a carelessly casual manner. Tonight, he fitted perfectly his role of Irish chieftain. He held himself with an unconscious arrogance, making her suddenly aware that he was an aristocrat, a man specially privileged by reason of character and birth to rule. Her heart raced as she slowly descended the stairs towards him. He looked grave as he watched her slender approaching figure, no teasing smile quirked his lips and the merry twinkle that had so often annoyed her with its inconsequence was completely absent from his eyes. When finally she reached him, he held out his hand to clasp hers and in complete silence they studied each other.

He was looking outstandingly handsome in an impeccably tailored evening suit, its blackness offset by a pristine linen shirt displaying cuffs held together by discreet diamond links. His unruly hair had been firmly disciplined, and a pleasant aroma drifted from the cheroot he had chosen in preference to his usual cigarette. He threw the half-smoked butt into the heart of the cavernous stone fireplace and drew her towards the warmth of a small sitting-room where a champagne bottle was frosting in an ice bucket and flames from the fire were being deflected in rainbow sparkles from a tray of tall-stemmed crystal goblets. With alien gravity, he told her, 'We have much to discuss. Later, when dinner is over, we will talk in here, alone, but just now I have to tell you one thing.'

When he paused Georgina mutely questioned him, somehow incapable of finding her voice. His hands reached out to close upon the smooth rounded warmth of her shoulders to pull her gently towards him.

'You're very beautiful, my darling, do you know that? How beautiful, I didn't really appreciate until a few moments ago when I watched you float down the stairs wrapped in a silver cloud. Don't make me wait too long for you, Gina, my love, I feel I've waited a lifetime already!'

His hand touched her shoulder in a light caress as his eyes under lowered lids said more than the words he whispered in her ear. Georgina told herself that beneath those limpid eyelids he was fully awake to the havoc he was causing, and she felt he deserved applause for the masterly way he had projected an undertone of sincerity into his words. She yearned to denounce him right there and then as a philandering cheat, to convince him with stormy words that his planned assault was having little or no effect upon her senses. Perhaps if she spoke she might, by the very sting of her words, also convince herself! Her own self-anger was so intense she had to struggle to hide it from him. He was so close, waiting for her answer, and she gave it by looking directly into his eyes and smiling with simulated tenderness. It was enough. When he lowered his head she called upon all her courage to help combat the havoc his kisses caused her, but she was saved that ordeal when Michael's impish voice spoke from somewhere behind them.

'I hope I'm not interrupting anything important, but Kate is anxious to begin serving dinner and as she has taken such pains with it, I'm sure you don't want to upset her by keeping her waiting.'

Lian scowled. His hands dropped to his sides as he turned upon the openly laughing Michael with mock ferocity.

'May the devil take you, Rooney, for your ill-timed appearance; whatever good qualities you might possess tact is not one of them! Still,' he offered Georgina his arm to lead her to the dining-room where an anxious Kate was hovering, 'perhaps it's for the best, for who knows how long we might have lingered if you hadn't made your unwelcome interruption. But I warn you, Michael, that immediately after dinner I shall expect you to disappear completely. Gina and I have many things to discuss before we can begin to make arrangements for our wedding, and your company will then be superfluous.' His grin removed all offence from these words, and Michael's answering, knowing smile sent the blood rushing to Georgina's face.

During dinner she found it an effort to keep up with Michael's exuberance and Lian's teasing quips. They both seemed determined to put her at her ease, but their methods only served to make her withdraw into a tight shell of composure inside of which she felt safe from their devastating battery of charm. She was determined not to weaken, and yet, as the meal progressed, she felt more than one fleeting pang of regret that she dared not allow herself to relax completely in their invigorating company. As one course followed another, they vied with each other to bring a smile or an answering tease to her lips, and were visibly puzzled when they failed. She was perfectly polite, listening intently to their remarks, and smiling her appreciation of Michael's jokes, but the sparkle was missing from her eyes and the wit from her answers. She felt Lian's intent look, and realized that she was toying with the food Kate had excelled herself in preparing. Hastily, she took a mouthful of the fairy-light lemon sponge on her plate to try to divert his attention from her lack of appetite, but when she looked up a second later he was frowning, obviously puzzled by her attitude.

Michael had no misgivings whatever, he was quite sure he knew what it was that was bothering his subdued niece. He looked from her to Lian and announced blithely:

'I know that look! It's the look of a business executive on holiday who's just beginning to start worrying about whether or not she's dispensable. Forget about Electronic International, alannah; let Stella and Whalley worry themselves into an early grave if they want to, but you must remember doctor's orders: complete rest, remember?'

Lian cut in, 'I refuse to believe Gina is so foolish as to worry about a business she will no longer have any interest in once we're married. She will discontinue all active participation in it then, as she will be busily occupied elsewhere, I promise you.'

His decree was so absolute, with no argument wanted or indeed expected, that Georgina's temper rose. She was not used to having decisions made for her and she resented the arbitrary way in which he had settled her life before even discussing it with her.

'But what if I say I want to continue with my job after our marriage?' she asked with deceptive meekness.

Lian regarded her unsmilingly, his eyes steady. 'Then I would tell you that it's out of the question,' he countered smoothly. 'Irishmen like to be the breadwinners of the family, just as they like their womenfolk to be the homemakers, and I'm no exception.'

When she gave a hard, derisive laugh his mouth tightened. Recklessly, she disregarded this danger signal and tilted scornfully:

'My mother and grandmother could give lie to

that sentiment, were they here. Each of them was married to an Irishman and they both lived to regret it!'

'May one ask why?' Lian's voice was austere.

Momentarily, she blanched, then blundered on, 'Because of their husbands' utter irresponsibility, their lack of moral fibre, and also, I suspect, because of an Irish characteristic which they possessed in abundance: laziness!'

Michael's face registered outraged dismay, but he recovered swiftly and roared across the table, 'Those are your mother's words, my girl, not yours, and they're lies, all lies!' He would have ranted on, but Lian interrupted him.

'As we have finished, Michael, perhaps you will excuse me if I ask you to leave us. I want to speak to Gina alone.' Michael was not too insensible to recognize the command behind the softly spoken request and he rose immediately, scowling blackly at Georgina as he did so.

'I'm going upstairs to pack a few things. I've arranged with Tom O'Connell to spend a few days fishing on Lough Derg, so I'll be leaving early in the morning. I hope,' he glared at Georgina before turning back to Lian, 'that by the time I return you'll have managed to instil some sense into my niece's head!'

There was silence when he left the room, a pregnant, brooding silence Georgina dared not break. She knew Lian was angry, and waited with clenched fists for his wrath to fall, only to be disconcerted when, in a perfectly controlled voice, he suggested, 'Shall we move into the sitting-room where we'll be more comfortable?' Without looking at him, she rose from the table and made her way to the adjacent room. She sat down near to the fire—she felt suddenly cold—and was put at an immediate disadvantage when he leant an elbow against the stone fireplace and towered over her.

She stared, fascinated, at the smoke curling from the banked-up peat, its heart smouldering with no less heat than that of the man who overshadowed her. She had not meant to choose this moment for her dénouement, her intention had been to lead him on for a few more days, up until the time of her departure, then when he was completely assured of his success, she would have shattered him completely. But she had not reckoned on nervous tension besetting her to the extent that it had, nor had she allowed for the treacherous feelings that turned hatred into yearning and willpower into weakness each time he touched her. Even though she despised herself for it, when he addressed her exclusively as 'Gina' her heart leapt with pleasure at the sound.

He, too, was gazing, deep in thought, into the heart of the fire, but he turned to her abruptly when he asked, 'Would you mind explaining to me your bitter indictment of my fellow-countrymen? I gather you have a very low opinion of Irishmen ... your grandfather ... and your father ... Am I also included among the men you so bitterly despise? How can you equate your resentment and contempt of Irishmen with your intention to marry one of the despised race? I'm presuming you have not forgotten that we're engaged ...'

She rose to her feet with a jerk that betrayed her

nervousness, but managed to meet his look bravely. Now that the moment was upon her, she intended to wring the most out of his discomfiture as a sort of compensation for the heartburning she herself had suffered.

'*I wouldn't marry you if you were the last man on earth!*' she enunciated clearly into the silence of the room.

Not by the flicker of an eyelid did he betray his surprise; he stood motionless and silent waiting for her to continue. 'I heard you,' she charged him fiercely, 'plotting with my uncle to flatter and cajole me into building our factory here in Kerry! I realized that night that everything my mother had said about the Irish was true; you're unscrupulous, idle wasters who would far rather sponge on some unsuspecting stranger than work out your own salvation. I suffered your unwanted attentions merely to trick you, as you would have tricked me, but I can assure you, Chief Ardulian, there will be no factory built here, so your efforts have all been in vain!'

While she spoke, Lian became progressively whiter until, as she finished, his face could have been etched in marble. Georgina, her slim body trembling with the force of her anger, swallowed hard and blinked away humiliating tears that threatened to fall, but as she could no longer trust her voice to remain steady she relapsed into a frustrated silence.

He straightened, squaring his shoulders as if accepting some unexpected burden. His voice rasped her quivering nerves when it was forced through lips so tight they seemed barely to move.

'Allow me to congratulate you. I thought Deirdre had a great deal of acting ability, but she couldn't enact a performance to equal yours. You're a loss to the theatre, Miss Rooney—never once during our love scenes did you allow your utter loathing of myself to show through! That, of course, could be due to your upbringing. Your uncle assured me, and I was fool enough to disregard him, that you were a hard-headed businesswoman entirely lacking in sentiment or feeling, but, *my God*, I can believe him now!

She flinched inwardly even while her head tilted in proud defiance, and saw his fists clench tightly as he battled for control. Fear knotted inside her at the sight of the barely restrained violence that tautened his frame. He towered over her like a bird of prey, his eagle's eyes piercing her pale face for some sign of penitence, but she stared back scornfully, praying that her veneer of confidence would not crack under the strain of knowing that she had crossed swords with a man of mercurial temperament, a man descended from a long line of reckless rebels who had refused to recognize, much less obey, any civilized code of conduct.

She found it a great effort to shrug and appear casual when she retorted, 'What you believe will not concern me for long, I intend to leave here as soon as possible.' Heavily sarcastic, she requested: 'Might I prevail further upon your hospitality by asking you to arrange for a car to take me to the nearest railway station tomorrow morning?'

Not daring to wait for an answer, she turned swiftly on her heel and almost ran from the room.

# CHAPTER SEVEN

WHEN she reached her room Georgina celebrated
her success by throwing herself on the bed, sobbing
bitterly. She could not understand why she should
feel so ashamed of her actions; he deserved to be
humiliated. But she knew the memory of his
shocked face, the incredulity and contempt she had
seen in his eyes, would haunt her for ever. She could
derive little comfort from the fact that he had
neither excused nor denied the behaviour she had
charged him with; most of his anger had seemed
to stem from the remarks she had made about his
countrymen in general and the knowledge that she
was aware of his own devious plans had seemed to
cause him the least concern.

When finally she undressed and climbed into bed
it was to face a night of tormenting thoughts,
thoughts that kept her wide awake until she heard
the first warbling bird greet the dawn with a song
of welcome she was unable to endorse; tortured
though the night had been, she would have suffered
it a hundred times rather than have to face Lian
Ardulian again.

Weary-eyed, and with a throbbing head, she
packed her things before going down to breakfast.
She ate alone. Michael, Kate informed her after
appraising her wan face, had departed at first light
with his fishing tackle and a change of clothing,

while Himself, who had also breakfasted early, had left a message that she was to be ready to leave around nine o'clock, at which time a car would be waiting.

Kate seemed to be of the opinion that an outing had been planned for that day, and Georgina decided it would be less painful if she made no mention of her departure. Already she felt a great fondness for the old lady, which she felt sure was reciprocated, but Kate's penchant for emotional scenes could be harrowing even when the occasion was a happy one, and she could not bear the thought of the climax that might be reached if she was made aware that this was to be their last meeting. She chatted bravely to cover up her lack of appetite until, just before nine, she rose from the table and kissed Kate lightly upon each cheek in her own private farewell of the kindly soul.

Kate flushed with pleasure and returned her kiss, even as, almost in one breath, she admonished, 'Now see that you take a coat with you when you go out, dearie, we've had exceptionally fine weather these last few days, but it won't last for much longer, I'm thinking, and it's better to be safe than sorry.'

'Yes, I'll do that, Kate,' Georgina smiled. 'It's so good of you to worry over me. Such a pleasant change ...' Her voice petered out, choked by an onrush of desolation.

'Go on with you,' Kate laughed, pleased. 'You'll never in your life be able with truth to say that again. Not if I know Himself as well as I think I do. Ah, here he is! To be sure he'll have a good laugh when I tell him what you've just said.'

'No, please!' Georgina gasped as her startled eyes saw Lian's tall figure appear unexpectedly in the doorway, but Kate was deaf to her plea.

'You're neglecting your future bride shamefully,' she chided him with the familiarity of one who had nursed him through every childhood illness. 'She's after becoming so depressed when you're out of her sight she nearly has a body sobbing, her saying things like: "Nobody cares enough to worry about me!" Did you ever hear the like?' she twinkled. 'I leave you to reassure her on that score.' She bustled out, leaving Georgina mortified.

Lian's face was inscrutable. Ignoring her flushed cheeks, he sauntered into the room and stated flatly:

'If you're ready, we'll go. I have a car outside.'

Still flustered, she made to pass him. 'I'll get my bag, it's in my room.'

His hand shot out to detain her. 'No need, I'll fetch it. Do you have a coat?'

'On the bed,' she stammered, achingly conscious of the coldness he was emitting, 'with gloves and a handbag.'

He took the stairs three at a time and seconds later returned carrying her things. Less than five minutes afterwards, she was sitting in the back of a surprisingly opulent car watching Eagles' Mount fade into the distance through a haze of quick tears.

They sped in silence through countryside that looked vaguely familiar. She recalled seeing some of the landmarks they passed on their last journey in the jaunting cart, but whereas on that occasion they had wandered along winding footpaths, this time he kept to the road and after a while the scenery became monotonous; flat bogland that seemed to stretch for miles inland, away from the beauty of the rugged coastline and the lofty peaks that sheltered the eagles of Ardulian. They, at least, would welcome the reprieve they had been given; as long as the region remained isolated they would make it their home. The mighty eagle had no place among factory buildings and the bustle of civilization: no more than had the man in front of her whose driving was receiving a rapt attention totally unneccessary on such deserted roads. He, also, was too wild and free to accept the shackles any business enterprise would be bound to bring in its wake.

After another few miles of silent progress she felt a stirring of unease. Surely, by now, she should be seeing some signs of habitation? She had no sense of direction to speak of, but instinct told her that no railway station would be found situated amid such barren desolation. Her nervous fingers mangled her gloves to a pulp before she found the courage to protest.

'Where are you taking me? This can't be the way to the railway station. I can see no tracks—no sign of habitation!'

He did not turn his head, but the hard determination she saw stamped upon his profile prepared her a little for his incredible answer.

'You're not going home just yet. I feel your education is in some respects incomplete and might benefit from a sojourn in less comfortable circumstances that those at Eagles' Mount!'

'I don't understand!' she gasped, unable to believe the threat in his words; surely he would not dare to carry out what would amount to an abduction! But fast on the heels of doubt came the memory of his family motto: We Dare All! words that concealed no idle threat, rather the reverse. Full of frightened desperation, she looked around for some avenue of escape, but there was none: even if she should succeed in jumping from the moving car there was nowhere to run to, no friendly human being to whom she might appeal for help.

Just then she caught sight of a blur in the distance which, as they moved nearer, began to take the shape of a white-walled cottage similar to that of Daniel Kavanagh's. A quick surge of hope lightened her spirits—here was deliverance if only it could be reached! With unforeseen luck, she felt the car slowing down and tensed, ready to leap out when the cottage came within running distance. As soon as she judged it was near enough, she flung open the car door and threw herself sideways, praying she would break no bones on impact. She landed with a thud that knocked her breathless. She was not hurt, but it was quite some seconds before she had recovered enough to begin an attempt to run towards the cottage.

The screech of brakes as Lian pulled up added impetus to her movements, but when she struggled to rise it was as if a thousand hidden hands held her relentlessly in their grip. Striving to overcome her panic, she projected all her strength behind her next attempt, but to her horror thick black slime oozed over her legs and she felt her body sink farther into what she now realized was a quaking expanse of bogland. Fear such as she had never before ex-

perienced shot through her body and a terrified
scream left her lips. During her childhood she had
heard tales in plenty from her father and uncle
about the peat bogs that could swallow a horse in
minutes and whose deceptive green covering had
served down the ages as a shroud for countless
numbers of unwary humans. The thought of such
a horrible death wrenched from her another
frightened scream that ended as a choke in her
throat when she saw Lian running towards her.

'You little fool!' he gritted when he reached her.
'I've a good mind to leave you there.'

'Oh, please, please hurry ...!' she begged. He
leant towards her, his hands outstretched, and her
terrified clasp almost precipitated him beside her
in the mire, but he swiftly recovered his balance
and heaved until the bog and she parted company
with a horrible sucking noise that sounded like the
deprived moan of some fearful monster.

Disregarding the thick black ooze that covered
her, she clung to him as if he were a life-line, shivering violently with shock, and forgetting entirely in
her relief at being rescued that he alone was responsible for her predicament. For seconds she clung to
him without speaking, then, her arms around his
neck, she felt him begin to shake. She had recovered
enough to feel swift compunction at what she
thought was his reaction to the shock of finding her
in such danger, and when she raised her head to reassure him she saw that his face was red and his lips
tightly clenched. Even as she began to commiserate,
he lost control and, to her incredulous fury, she saw
him fold up helplessly, convulsed with laughter.

She stared, amazed by his swift transition from grimness to amusement—his volatile emotions could fluctuate from one extreme to the other with the fluidity of quicksilver—and watched mortified as tears rolled down his cheeks while he roared with laughter. She could have derived much pleasure from assaulting him physically, but sensed that such punitive action would only accelerate his amusement, so she waited, visibly fuming, until his laughter was spent.

It was some time before he was able to control himself sufficiently to apologize, and when he eventually did his words sounded so supiciously meek she knew he was still fighting an uncontrollable urge to laugh. Wooden-faced, she stared at him as he choked out:

'I'm sorry, it's unforgivable of me I know, but if you could only see yourself . . .!'

He took a deep breath to help maintain his control, but a wide grin refused to be suppressed when his eyes travelled once more over her mud-caked figure. She could have wept with frustration. She knew she looked a sight, but that was nothing to the way she felt. Slime was running down the back of her neck, her feet squelched inside shoes full of the revolting stuff, and damp had saturated her clothing so much that she could feel the chill penetrating her very bones. Her spirited reply:

'Please think nothing of it, I'm glad you find me so amusing!' was spoiled by a shiver she could not control. Immediately full of remorse, he cursed himself for a fool.

'You must get out of those wet things before you

catch your death.' He moved quickly into action and with one stride narrowed the gap between them. For a second as he hovered over her, she had no idea what to expect, and edged nervously away, but then she found herself plucked from the ground, cradled in strong arms, and borne with effortless haste in the direction of the cottage.

No one stirred as they neared the cottage; no welcoming figure appeared at the doorway to bid them enter, and it was only when Lian reached into his pocket for a key which, when he fitted it into the lock, worked perfectly, that she began to suspect that the cottage—so similar to the other cottages dotted around the countryside—might be the home of the Kavanaghs.

Once inside, she had no further doubt, the impoverished interior was etched upon her memory. Deirdre had lavished paint, many colours of brilliant paint, over the staircase, doors, and windowsills, but its smooth application only highlighted the poor quality of the wood it covered and the light colours served to emphasize the yawning gaps that gave access to draughts that pierced through the ill-fitting doors. No fire was lighted in the empty grate, so as soon as Lian set her down, he strode towards a wooden chest, pulled out a blanket, and ordered her: 'Get out of those wet things and wrap this around you until I get a fire going.' He frowned. 'What you really need is a hot bath, but as it will be quite some time before the water is heated you'll have to make do with a good rub down. At least you have something to change into, once the fire is going,

I'll fetch your stuff from the car.'

'Th ... thank you ...' she replied through chattering teeth, 'but I must have a wash, even if I have to use cold water. Where is the bathroom?'

He glinted down at her with some form of enjoyment and replied suavely, 'There isn't one.'

'No bathroom?' Her voice was incredulous.

'No bathroom, no electricity, not even piped water,' he challenged grimly. 'Here, perhaps, you'll begin to understand what I mean when I say you might benefit from a spell in less comfortable circumstances than you've been used to hitherto. Just imagine, Miss Rooney,' she flinched at the mockery in his voice, 'if it were not for the fact that your grandfather emigrated when he did, you too could have been born and reared in a cottage similar to this one where, if you want a bath, or even a cup of tea, you have to take a bucket and walk to the nearest spring for water!'

Georgina drew in a quick breath at the implication behind his words. Was he seriously considering keeping her here in these primitive conditions in order to punish her for her sharp indictment of his people? With his highly developed sense of the ridiculous it was more than likely!

Anxiety sharpened her tone as she asked, 'Where are the Kavanaghs? You'll never persuade them to keep me here against my will!'

He nodded his agreement. 'I'm aware of that. That's why I waited until they'd gone.'

Her frightened eyes swept the room as if she expected the absent Kavanaghs to appear from out of the woodwork. 'Gone ... gone where? I don't be-

93

lieve you. Deirdre told me that Daniel has never been out of this valley in his life, so he'd hardly agree to leave it now!' She shivered again, not with cold but with fear, and Lian, who had turned to attend to the fire, looked up just in time to see it.

'We'll leave the questions until later,' he ordered sharply. 'Don't stand there shivering, get those wet things off immediately!'

At the arrogance of his command, her head jerked up and she retorted with spirit, 'I don't intend to budge until you've told me what I want to know. Where are Deirdre and Daniel?'

With a muttered imprecation, he left the fire and strode over to grab her by the shoulders. 'All right, you stubborn little devil, I'll tell you. Daniel has gone to London. After much pleading by Deirdre, and a rattling good talking to from myself, he's been persuaded to go into hospital to have an eye operation to remove cataracts which were threatening to send him blind. Deirdre arranged it all months ago, but Daniel flatly refused to leave because there was no one to look after the animals and his few crops. Deirdre appealed to me for help, and by promising Daniel I would send a man to look after things here, we managed to get him to reconsider. However,' his eagle eyes pierced her, 'I decided not to send a man, but to come myself and to bring you with me. I know that you, with your cool business brain and first-class capabilities, will have this place ticking over in no time. Now is your chance to show us idle, lazy Irishmen how to organize our assets so that they become profitable propositions. This smallholding is typical of many in Kerry, and that's why I've brought you here. I'll be waiting with breathless interest for your summing up as to where we go wrong in our business methods and for your solution to the problem of how to wring a living from two inches of topsoil and acres of barren rock! Now,' he shook her fiercely, 'you have exactly five minutes to get out of those wet clothes. If you're not rid of them by then I'll remove them myself!'

Angrily he strode outside and left her alone to grapple with a dozen conflicting emotions. Her hands shook as she removed her caked clothes which by now were half dried upon her back. Her confused mind could not grasp the significance of all the words he had ejected with such fiercely held control; only one fact had registered: he was not engaged to Deirdre. The meeting she had built up in her mind as being an application to Daniel for permission to marry had all the time been nothing more than a ploy to get Daniel into hospital.

She had to rub herself vigorously to remove the worst of what remained of the mud, but her exertion had nothing to do with the heat that sent blood rushing to her cheeks. She was remembering the dreadful things she had accused him of in her mind. How could she have imagined it would be possible for him to keep secret the fact that he had become engaged to both Deirdre and herself at one and the same time? Common sense told her, too late, that such a scheme was totally alien to the proud chief of Ardulian whose most outstanding quality was the honour in which he held his name.

She was almost sobbing with frustration, caused not wholly by her unsuccessful efforts to get herself clean, when he knocked and shouted outside the door:

'I've brought you your suitcases, can I come in?'

Her voice quavered as she clutched the blanket around her and stepped forward to answer. 'I refuse to get dressed with all this dirt on me, I must have a wash. Can't you *please* get me some water?'.

'I'm sorry,' came the implacable answer, 'I have other work to do, you'll have to get some yourself. Surely,' his voice was edged with impatience, 'you can pull on some slacks and a jumper for the time being? A peck of dirt won't harm you!'

Georgina swallowed her angry reply. He was odious! He took her silence for agreement and opened the door just wide enough to push her cases through. Shivering with fastidious distaste, she pulled clean underclothes from her suitcase and began to dress. Whatever happened, she vowed through clenched teeth, she would have her bath, even if it meant plunging into a cold stream. The sound of cheerful whistling as Lian went about his chores lent fuel to her fury, a fury that hardened into a resolve that, come what may, he was not going to break her spirit. She was an American, pioneer stock on her mother's side, and no Irish rebel was going to grind her nose into the dust!

# CHAPTER EIGHT

FIVE minutes later, feeling filthier than she had ever felt in her life before, Georgina went in search of Lian. She had the foresight to pick up the two metal buckets she saw standing empty by the side of the flat stone slab that served as a sink, and when she finally found him feeding two pigs at the back of the house she rattled the buckets and demanded haughtily, 'Where do I go to fill these?'

He took his time straightening, then waved a cursory hand in the direction of a well trodden path leading away from the house and disappearing under a hedge. 'Up the bochareen. Just follow your nose, you can't miss it.'

'Thank you!' The same nose went up in the air, denoting her displeasure at his lack of courtesy. She would have died rather than plead with him to fetch the water, but as she stomped away in the direction he had indicated indignation was written in every line of her body.

She had no idea what a bochareen was, or looked like, but she walked along the path until she came to the hedge. There was a gap through which the path continued along a narrow lane winding between straggling, untrimmed hedges. She began to pant as the ground started to rise slightly, but the faint tinkling of water coming from a nettle-filled ditch alongside her denoted that she was on the right track, so she struggled on.

Then the path petered out, and she was left staring around at rock, fern, and weed—but no water. She stood still and listened, the sound of running water was aggravatingly close, but there was absolutely no sign of it. For all of half an hour she searched, telling herself that never again would she take for granted that vital commodity. Although she had rubbed herself sore in her attempt to get rid of the bog mud, its smell still lingered in her nostrils and she knew she would not be able to relax until the last remnant of it had been washed away. Nettles stung her legs as she blundered through thick undergrowth, and brambles tore at her clothing and scratched her face, but she continued her search, muttering scathing condemnation of Lian Ardulian as she did so.

She could have cried with vexation when finally she had to admit defeat. She stumbled over to a flat rock and sat with glazed eyes staring around at the camouflaging vegetation that was keeping its secret so well. At the thought of having to go back to the cottage empty-handed, a sob escaped her. How he would enjoy the sight of her misery; how he would gloat when once again he was given the opportunity to thrust down her throat the harsh conditions that were endured by the people she had scorned as lazy! She was sorry for the things she had said, and was now beginning to realize that the poverty that existed in the Gaeltacht was in no way the fault of the people who endured its rigours. Also, she had a feeling Lian Ardulian was going to show her no mercy during her forced stay, his intention was to ensure that when she left this region it would be with either a firm resolve to help do what she could to alleviate distress or, failing that, with a conscience so heavily laden with guilt she would never again enjoy peace of mind.

She sat with bowed head, nerving herself to begin the return journey. Dejectedly, she swiped at a clump of tall ferns and she was just about to rise to go on her way when her eye caught a quick flash of silver. Hardly able to believe her luck, she leant forward, brushing aside more fern, and there in front of her she saw a pool about twenty inches wide, dark, unmoving, but crystal clear. With a shout of pure joy, she knelt and cupped her hands in its cool depths, raising the nectar to her lips, its ice-cold tastelessness chilling her tongue. After drinking deeply, she filled her buckets to the brim and began retracing her steps to the cottage, feeling so triumphant that the weight she carried went unnoticed.

Lian was throwing grain to a horde of squawking chickens when Georgina staggered the last few yards to the house. A fugitive smile twitched at the corner of his mouth when he threw away the last handful and moved forward to meet her.

'I thought you were lost,' he offered blandly, 'did you have difficulty in finding the spring?'

Aware that he was laughing at her, she tilted her chin and lied, 'Not a bit, it was so peaceful up there I just sat for a while and ... and thought,' she finished defiantly.

'Ah,' he replied, tongue in cheek, 'I understand, it's good to find a spot where the heart can be tranquil. I hope your thoughts were pleasant ones?'

Angrily she turned away from his mockery, but as she walked away she questioned frigidly across her shoulder, 'Would you mind showing me how I'm to heat the water? If I don't get this filth off me I'll scream!'

Perhaps he realized he was driving her too hard, or maybe it was that her defiant words did not completely hide the dejection she was feeling. His voice was suddenly kind when he answered:

'Here, give those buckets to me. I can't guarantee you a hot bath, but if I pour this lot into what Deirdre calls her "witch's cauldron" and heat it over the fire there'll be enough, with another couple of bucketsful added, to ensure you a lukewarm one.'

Deirdre's witch's cauldron turned out to be a great iron pot with a half hoop across its top which Lian hooked on to a bar slung across the now glowing fire. He emptied the water into it, and before setting out to the spring to refill the buckets, he dragged from an outhouse a zinc bath which he placed in front of the fire.

'There, milady,' he grinned, 'your bath is almost ready.'

When she looked askance around the bare room, he read her thoughts and told her dryly, 'Don't worry about the lack of privacy. I have some ploughing to do before dark, so when your bath is ready I'll get on with it. It should take me at least two hours,' he stressed. She blushed, his perception was uncanny, but before she could collect her thoughts he picked up the buckets and strode out of the cottage.

She revelled in her bath to such an extent she

lost all track of time. Never before had the ritual she had pursued every day of her life given her so much relief and pleasure. Her bathroom back home was a symphony in blue; blue bath, blue-tiled walls with mirror insets, enormous fluffy pale-blue towels, and glass shelves filled with every conceivable toilet requisite. But she had never spared any more than ten minutes at a time inside its luxurious interior, the everlasting flow of steaming water had hardly been noted, its value to her being merely functional.

Here the water was barely six inches deep, luke-warm and cooling rapidly. The zinc bath was ridged at the bottom, making it impossible to retain a comfortable position for any length of time, and the heat from the fire, although welcome, was fairly roasting one side of her while her opposite side was being chilled by a draught that whistled through the cracks in the door. Nevertheless, it was heaven to soap her body with a thick wedge of carbolic that stung her nostrils with its astringency and to rinse away every last lingering trace of bog mud.

When she had towelled dry and the clothes she had been wearing had been cast aside for fresh ones, she experienced such a sense of well-being that she felt the trials she had endured might almost have been worthwhile; in the same context that pain is worthwhile if only for the exquisite pleasure experienced when it finally disappears.

By the time she had emptied the bath and returned it to the outhouse, she was ravenous. Lunch-time had passed without food being mentioned by Lian and as pride would not allow her to plead with him for food, she had tightened her belt and forced herself not to think about eating. But her hunger was now past bearing, so she hurried inside the cottage and began to forage in the hope of finding enough stores to provide a meal. All she found was a dish of butter and some potatoes, but even these basic items were enough to set her mouth watering. She peeled enough potatoes for two—she could hardly miss him out even if he did deserve to starve —and put them into the pan of water that had been left heating over the fire. She seasoned them with salt, then gently placed another piece of turf on top of the glowing pile. It was not long before the potatoes were bubbling gently, and while she waited for them to cook she spread a chequered cloth on the bare wooden table and set two places for the meal.

She was humming quietly, bending over the pan to test the potatoes for eating, when Lian returned to the cottage. His entry was so quiet that when his voice reached across her shoulder she swung round, startled, and in her confusion dropped the fork.

'Congratulations,' he mocked. 'I would never have believed you capable of cooking potatoes. Would your business associates recognize you now, I wonder?' He bent down to pick up the fork while he waited for her answer.

To hide her confusion she spoke with asperity. 'I wish they were here to answer that question for themselves, but as they aren't perhaps we can eat. I'm famished!' He glanced over to the table where the dish of butter took pride of place and then at the pan of potatoes, and his eyebrows tilted. But he sat down without a word and waited to be served.

They ate in unsociable silence; she too hungry to spare time for speech, and he engrossed in thoughts of his own, thoughts that furrowed his brow and clouded his face in morose shadow. But when Georgina pushed her empty plate away, feeling replete enough to begin demanding explanations, he leant back against his chair, lighted a cigarette, and met her eyes with a challenge that told her he was more than prepared to meet her arguments.

Nervously she cleared her throat before asking, 'Do you seriously intend keeping me here against my will, or are your actions simply bluff—an attempt to frighten me into agreeing to bring industry here? If it is the latter, then I can assure you it won't work, anyone who knows me well will tell you I can be persuaded but never coerced!' she finished defiantly.

Her blood chilled when he answered, 'My actions are intended neither as bluff nor as intimidation, but are intended simply to teach you a well-deserved lesson; to help you to remember in future that all is not what it seems on the surface. Just as the bog you jumped into looked at first sight deceptively firm and healthy, there are other situations about which you know equally little but upon which you don't hesitate to pass judgement. In years to come you will be grateful to me for filling a gap in your education which seems to have been overlooked by whoever was responsible for your upbringing.'

His cool cheek took her breath away, and for a moment all she could do was glare at him across the sparsely filled table. Then, 'You're insufferable!'

she spat at him. 'Thank goodness our engagement was a farce, I should hate to even pretend to be engaged to a man full of such presumptuous arrogance!'

'The engagement stands!' His cool tone matched the blue icicles glinting in his eyes and froze into silence her hot answering retort. He watched her through narrowed eyes and continued, 'Although our engagement was never officially announced, by now news of it will have spread right across the county. I do not intend to be made the target of gossip-mongers, nor will I allow the name of Ardulian to be held up to ridicule, so, whether you like it or not, you will remain my fiancée until I consider enough time has elapsed between the announcement of our engagement and the termination of it to ensure that there's no speculation.'

She jerked upright, two bright flags of colour burning her cheeks. '*You* are concerned about gossip! You who are holding me here against my will, without the presence of any kind of chaperone to help still chattering tongues! I don't understand your reasoning at all. Which do you think will cause the most gossip, a broken engagement, or our stay here alone in the depths of nowhere without a soul to ensure that the proprieties your people place so much importance upon are being observed?'

Her heated words had no effect upon his implacability. He seemed almost bored with the conversation when he stubbed out his cigarette and told her, 'No one ever passes this way by chance, if they come at all it's to visit Daniel, and as everyone knows he's away just now, they won't be likely to make the journey, especially when they know there won't be the reward of even a cup of tea at the end of it. As far as Daniel's friends are concerned the house is deserted, so you needn't worry about being discovered.'

'There's my Uncle Michael,' she thrust back, incensed. 'Not even he would allow you this much rope!'

'He's miles away, fishing, and before you mention Kate, I can tell you now that I dropped her a hint that we might be joining him for a few days, so that when we don't return this evening she'll think, with an easy mind, that that's what we've decided to do.'

Georgina's indignant colour slowly faded, leaving her pale and anxious. Her smoke-grey eyes widened as unconsciously she pleaded with him to deny his rigid pronouncements, but there was no softening in the inflexible look that impaled her heart and left it quivering as if flicked with the tip of cold steel. He meant every word he said, of that there was no doubt—the eagle was no longer hooded! A shiver of apprehension ran through her as she thought of the eagles mounting guard around his home; just like those wild creatures, he too was of the nature to turn against those who sought to thwart him.

The scrape of his chair against the stone floor startled her so much that her body jerked visibly. Now that she knew the extent of his ruthlessness, the lonely farmhouse and its solitary surroundings had taken on a sinister aspect in her frightened mind which was sending danger signals tingling down her spine. When he towered over her, she gave an involuntary gasp and cowered back in her chair. He stepped nearer to look down at her, his expression unfathomable, and again she shrank back.

She felt hysteria rise inside her as he stood immobile in the lengthening silence. The gay charmer whose inconsequential nature she had felt confident she could manipulate had completely disappeared; the grim stranger who had taken his place represented a greater challenge than any she had ever encountered. In the business world, where she had cut her first teeth on her mother's gold-plated executive's pen and where her first words had been an echo of her mother's, uttered in the cut-and-thrust vernacular of a business woman making known her ability to compete in a man's world, she had reigned supreme. But before Lian Ardulian she felt stripped of all assurance. The cool composure she had striven for years to develop faded like mist from a mountain top when she tried to pit her puny strength against his superior personality. This was the thing that frightened her more than any other; her mother had bolstered her ego to such an extent she had felt herself capable of outwitting any man, but here, away from the reassuring solidity of Electronic International, she was left feeling weakly feminine and completely helpless when opposed by the man who refused to accord her the deference which, as her mother's daughter, she had become accustomed.

She passed a weary hand across her brow, she was tired, it had been a long, eventful day and dusk was closing in around the silent farmhouse. What else did he intend asking of her? What further plan to humiliate was being devised behind the silent mask that was animated only by deep blue eyes that for minutes had been closely scrutinizing her? She had to know.

Abruptly she asked, 'Where do I sleep?' and was surprised by the meek diffidence of her voice.

He brooded down upon her. 'The bedroom's upstairs,' he jerked his head in the direction of an open staircase ascending the far wall. Her heart sank at the singular emphasis, but she mustered her courage and turned towards the stairs.

'Then if you don't mind, I'll say goodnight, I'm very tired.'

He put out a detaining hand. 'I'll go first,' he insisted smoothly. 'I'm familiar with the house, you might stumble in strange suroundings.' She made no demur when he went on ahead, but cold fingers clutched at her heart, causing a sensation of fear that paralyzed her breathing so much she had to fight to gulp in air through a tight throat.

It was much darker at the top of the stairs, where a windowless passage held only one door giving access to the solitary bedroom. He opened it with a flourish, shedding light into the passageway, and she stepped past him into the room. Inside was an iron bedstead with the thinnest mattress she had ever seen laid bare across its springs. Brass knobs, badly bulged, decorated the bed-ends with pathetic splendour, and a table with legs so rickety they seemed in danger of collapsing under the weight of its marble top, held a jug and matching washbasin.

She had seen these primitive washing utensils before, at home in America, in the homes of friends who had bought them as souvenirs of their trips to the 'old country'. There they were used to hold flower arrangements, or potted plants, and as such they were greatly admired and sought after, but how many people, Georgina wondered dully, would relish the thought of actually having to use them for the purpose for which they were originally intended?

Her incredulity must have shown, because Lian's voice echoed with mockery when he charged her:

'Primitive, isn't it?'

She turned swiftly, then backed away from his nearness. He was leaning against the door jamb, his arms folded across his chest, his tall frame reaching intimidatingly high into the small room. Her one step away brought her hard up against the iron bedstead and, too late, she realized she was trapped. Mesmerized with fear, she watched his dark head lower towards her and heard him whisper meaningfully, 'But we are a primitive people, Miss Georgina Rooney, as perhaps you are becoming aware. I can imagine the thoughts that even now are churning through your frightened little mind. What is the Irish savage going to do next? Is he civilized enough to respect my dependence upon him, or does the blood of barbarians still run hot in his veins?'

He was tormenting her with all the enjoyment of a cruel child who has tied a can to a cat's tail, but whereas a child might be excused for its thoughtlessness, he could not be. Georgina's brave spirit rose in revolt, and when she challenged him her eyes were sparkling with angry defiance.

'Judging from past experience I would be a fool

to expect either consideration or decency from you. Any man who, like you, would involve himself with a woman purely for his own gain has to be devoid of all finer feelings. My mother's judgement has always been sound and, once again, her words have been proved right: *an Irishman should never be trusted*!'

The white line around his tight lips betrayed his fierce anger, but she did not flinch or try to evade his eyes when he gritted, 'Twice you've laid that charge against me, and I very much resent it!'

'But it's one you don't deny!' she flashed back.

'And never will,' he clamped, 'because to regard it at all would be to give to it an importance it doesn't deserve. I reject it as beneath contempt!'

As he glowered at her, Georgina's assurance faltered. Could she have been wrong about his motives? Her accusation had aroused his anger to such an extent he seemed visibly to be fighting to control it. Then she remembered the evidence of her own ears, the words spoken between himself and her uncle were carved indelibly on her mind—*hard-headed tycoon type ... sexless computer*—she flinched inwardly. With a set face, she condemned him, 'You prevaricate, Chief Ardulian, but unfortunately for you, I'm not quite the fool you take me for!'

He stiffened. She gave a gasp of alarm when his hand thrust out and closed around her arm in a grip that burned.

'You really believe I made love to you—asked you to become my wife—simply for the sake of money?'

The little room was as silent as a tomb while he

waited for her answer. As so often happens in moments of nervous tension, she fixed her eyes on an inanimate object—one of the brass knobs that decorated the bed—and concentrated upon it to the exclusion of everything else. But he refused to be excluded.

'Answer me!' He shook her vigorously.

She withstood his glare for half a second, but dropped her eyes when she jerked out, 'Yes, I do!'

She would have retracted immediately the words were spoken, but there was no going back. She saw from his set face that her suspicions had insulted him deeply; so deeply that when he answered it was as if iron had bit into his soul.

'So be it! I can see I would be wasting my time to attempt to change your opinion of me.' He nodded towards a solitary cupboard. 'The bed linen is in there. I shall be in the hay-loft if you should want me.'

A second later he had gone, his footsteps resounding on the bare boards of the staircase, and she was left staring around the room with a sinking feeling of desolation in her heart.

# CHAPTER NINE

THE nature of Ireland's climate is as inclement as that of its people. When the sun smiles upon the land, softening the harsh outlines of its peaks with its soft glow, and its lakes reflect blue brilliance from cloudless skies, contentment and tranquillity seem an integral ingredient of the perfect whole. But when the land, like its volatile inhabitants, suddenly erupts into tempest and storm, the outcome is frightening in the extreme. Winds blow straight from the Atlantic, springing up without warning to create havoc along the west coast. No place is immune from the rain-laden gusts that seek out even the most secluded corners as if grimly determining that no hidden cranny shall escape its baptism of wind and water. Bays around the coast become invisible as spray from the boiling sea is caught up and borne inshore on the passionate surge of the gale to form a mist-grey smoke-screen so impenetrable that all landmarks are lost beneath it. And to be caught in the wind means the terrible experience of having to place a calculated step upon a certain spot on the ground while at the same time throwing all the weight of the body forward against the onslaught to maintain balance.

The weather broke that night while Georgina lay restlessly courting sleep in the austere comfort of a strange bed. Her first intimation of the storm's advance came when a low grumble of thunder set the house trembling. She sat up quickly, her eyes flying instantly to the uncurtained window just in time to see a jagged streak of lightning, accompanied by a whipcrack noise, light up the room. She tensed, and jumped from the bed when, with a roar of gathering fury, the wind began tearing at the thatched roof, dislodging a cloud of dust particles that drifted slowly downwards to settle in a fine layer over everything in the room. With awakening panic, she scrambled into her clothes, flinching each time a flash of lightning illuminated the room, and trying hard to shut her ears against the demoniacal fury of wind and rain that was besieging the old farmhouse on all sides.

Now she was in a ferment of fear. Nothing previously had prepared her for the holocaust unleashed so suddenly on her unsuspecting head. She would have ridiculed any notion that she was afraid of storms, but witnessing the elements at work when inside the solidly constructed comfort of a New York office block, or inside the sound-proofed, air-conditioned apartment where she lived, was very different from being caught up in the heart of a tempest with only flimsy walls and an insubstantial thatched roof for protection.

She grabbed her coat and ran from the bedroom which now seemed to hold an atmosphere of menace. Even downstairs, each antiquated object ranged around the room, shrouded in shadow, seemed to glower intimidatingly down at her so that she fancied the room was filled with an aura of morose disapproval of her presence. Another clap of thunder, directly above, set the ground shuddering so violently she was petrified, but when white-hot lightning speared outside the window, searching for a victim, she jerked back to life and sprinted towards the door with a hysterical disregard for the dangers she would face outside.

'*Lian!*' Her shrill appeal was demolished by the howling wind as soon as it left her lips. The hay-loft, where he had said he would be sleeping, was only a few yards from the house. She ran out into the darkness, her eyes fixed on the void where she thought it would be, and felt herself lifted by the almost tangible wind and thrown violently back against the side of the house. Desperately she tried again, determined not to go back inside. She edged her way inch by inch along the wall, a feat that taxed her so much that she had to pause to gather strength before making a second attempt. The rain lashed down upon her slight figure with cold, stabbing fingers, but she would not be beaten into submission. When the wind died for an infinitesimal second, she was ready, and projected herself with all her strength in the direction of the hay-loft. She knew, with unshakable confidence, that her only salvation lay with Lian Ardulian; only he had the strength, the assurance, not only to win the fight against the elements but to revel in doing so.

Her flight came to an abrupt stop when she blundered full tilt into a hard, black object that first of all reeled away, then staggered back towards her. All the breath was knocked from her body at the moment of impact and she would have fallen if a grip of steel had not fastened upon her arms. A blessedly familiar voice yelled in her ear: 'You little fool, why didn't you stay in the house where it's safe!'

'*Lian! Oh, Lian!*' She collapsed sobbing against his chest, her tears mingling with the rain that soaked his coat, her frightened hands clutching him with an intensity that made him immediately aware of her terror. Swiftly he swung her off her feet and carried her to the hay-loft.

It was a mere framework, just a roof and two walls made of corrugated iron fitted together on the wind-ward side to protect the hay that was stacked three-quarters of the way up its sides. The remaining two sides were open to the gale, and the noise as the rain ricocheted off the metal was deafening. But Lian was there, holding her in the circle of his arms, so that even in the midst of the holocaust she felt, for some insane reason, perfectly secure.

She was still clinging to him, pressing her face against his coat which smelled of damp wool, when he shouted against her ear, 'Do you think you can stand the trip back to the house, there's no protection here?'

She lifted her head from his chest, intending to shout back that nothing would induce her to return there alone and that she would go only if he in-tended to remain with her, but when she looked up into his rain-streaked face her glance fastened with his. His black hair was rioting over his head, falling in wet spirals across his forehead so that he had to shake his head vigorously to rid himself of the drops caught in the thick tangle of lashes that framed his eyes. The sound of the storm faded as she stood staring up at him through the veiling gloom. Suddenly she had become overwhelmingly conscious of their closeness—his arms circling her waist; her hands clasping him so tightly she could feel the pattern of his heartbeat.

In that same second, he too became aware of her awareness and he caught his breath in a half-smothered gasp. Steadily, even as the storm raged around them, they stared at each other with cautious, exploratory wonder. Impelled by a primitive force, she surrendered to the delicious feeling of excitement that stole over her. Suspicion and all harsh thoughts fled from her mind as, with unwilling insight, she recognized the truth she had tried so long to subdue: she was attracted to the man she ought to hate; the man who earlier had made no secret of his own contempt of herself!

The elements raging around were no more savage than the emotions that were born as she trembled under his searching, alert eyes. He peered down through the darkness, trying to discover from her expression confirmation of the message betrayed by her pliant body. She did not stir from his tightening arms, but allowed a soft contented sigh to escape her. His quick ears caught the sound and with a smothered groan his endurance snapped. His hand reached out to tilt her chin, then, without waiting for any further reaction, his mouth swooped down to claim the kisses she had no will to withhold.

She had never experienced rapture until that moment. His earlier kisses had thrilled and disturbed her enough to make her regret the suspicions that lay between them, but now, in her weakened state, she surrendered wholly to the attraction he held for her and was transported on eagle's wings to heights she had never dreamed possible. As she softly murmured his name and stroked loving fingers through his black, tangled hair, the sound, low as it was, broke the bonds of inherited passion unimpaired even throughout generations of enforced civilization. He gathered her closer, his strong arms enfolding her like great eagle's wings, and plundered her mouth with kisses as savagely thrilling as any his wild Celtic ancestors might have bestowed upon the women they had abducted from the camps of their enemies; sometimes as an act of revenge, but more often through sheer devilment and love of excitement.

As his passion was unleashed, Georgina was swept up on its tide, happily and gloriously aware that she was in danger of drowning in a sea of turbulent feeling, but too completely overpowered to care. Her body pleaded for his touch as she pressed closer against his hard strength, her bones melted with tenderness as he caressed her, her mouth was sweetly and passionately pliable beneath his.

'*Gina!*' His voice was husky when he murmured into her hair then, again, his breath gently teasing her ear as his lips feathered across her cheek seeking another resting place: 'Gina, mavourneen, I want you so much ...!'

If she had not been so completely lost, then was the time to have withdrawn, but with reckless abandon she underlined her surrender in the indefinable way a woman can, without words, but with supplication in her eyes and yearning emanating from every nerve of her body.

The howling tempest surrounding them was a suitable accompaniment to the wild, surging passion that held them in its sway. Beads of sweat stood out on Lian's brow and small forks of lightning were reflected deep in the wild darkness of his eyes. Then, just when it seemed they would be swept beyond the bounds of sanity, he became suddenly still. She murmured her dissent when his arms dropped from around her. She reached out for him when he withdrew, and was upset when he set her at arm's length and regarded her steadily, his jaws tightly clamped.

'Lian . . .?' she questioned with pleading bewilderment.

His face whitened and the hands that held her tightened unbearably on her shoulders, making her share unknowingly in his frustration. 'We're going back to the house,' he grated, the coldness of his words belied by the damped-down ardour still visible in his eyes.

'But why, Lian?' She did not want to leave the heaven of his arms, not even for the short time it would take them to reach the house.

'Because we're going back to Eagles' Mount immediately.'

She was not allowed to voice a protest. Even as her passion-kissed lips formed the beginning of a pout, she was hustled out of the hay-shed to face the full force of the still raging storm. She needed all her breath to battle her way across to the cottage; the short journey was a nightmare even with his strong arms supporting her. The cottage door was open, as she had left it, and the force of the wind practically threw them into the kitchen. It seemed to howl with injustice when Lian forced back the door, shutting out the noisy elements and leaving them cocooned together in the dim, unlighted room.

Georgina moved towards him, impatient to be in his arms again, but he made no attempt to reciprocate when she folded her arms around his neck and lifted her mouth for his kiss. With eyes closed expectantly, she waited for what seemed an eternity, then, to her mortification she heard him say flatly, 'I'll get your suitcase,' before moving away.

Colour flooded her face when she opened her eyes and she saw his indifferent—almost bored—expression. But she had no pride left, and huskily she questioned the hurt he had inflicted, 'Lian, don't you ... want me any more?'

With a granite-hard profile, he stabbed out, 'I never did. I was experimenting, and now that I've proved my point I'm no longer interested!'

A chill crept over her, but she had to force him to continue. Running her tongue over suddenly dry lips, she asked, 'Would you explain, please ... I'm afraid I don't understand.'

He shrugged and stepped away so that his voice reached her from out of the darkness. 'I wanted to find out whether you really were as frigid and unresponsive as your uncle maintained you were.' If he heard her small gasp of hurt he made no sign, but went on deliberately to tear her heart to pieces. 'Yesterday you made a great show of being warm and womanly, but that was an act put on especially to lead me into a trap. What I really wanted to know was whether you had soul ... real genuine feelings

... or whether you're as cold and unfeeling as you're reputed to be.'

She closed her eyes the better to bear the bitter twisting pain that assaulted her. Shame. Humiliation. He had repaid her in full for daring to trick him, but she did not blame him so much as she blamed herself, her pitifully weak self. She could have sworn that this time his feelings had been genuine. Everything had happened so suddenly, so entirely without volition, that she could hardly take in the truth of his staggering rejection.

Tears blinded her as, with a sob he could not fail to hear, she challenged him, 'And *are* you convinced? If you are, would you please tell me your verdict, as,' a shaky laugh escaped her, 'for my own sake and for the sake of any future husband, I'd like to know!'

He was silent for so long she thought he did not intend to answer. When he eventually did, his voice was low and bitingly angry, but she somehow sensed that his anger was not directed entirely towards herself.

'I must admit to having been totally misinformed. You're all woman—a most attractive, very desirable woman—and you'll make an ideal mate for any man you might some day bring yourself to *trust*!'

She stared across the blackness that divided them, a blackness that cloaked his expression but which did not cover up the element of raw feeling stretching between them. She tried to project scorn into her answer, but only succeeded in faltering, 'So it was all pretence ... It was all a game to you, a despicable game of tit for tat.'

'Exactly,' his answer was projected clearly across the room. 'Yesterday was your day for games. today is mine. What a pity,' he taunted, 'we can't agree upon a time and place. The outcome would be most rewarding!' As if impatient of the whole thing, he moved towards the stairs and spoke sharply. 'We've continued with this abortive conversation long enough. I'll get your things and then we'll make off. The storm seems to be abating so, with luck, we should reach Eagles' Mount just a little after midnight, not too late for even Kate's sense of propriety.' He bounded up the stairs as if glad of any action to occupy him physically, and left her staring vacantly into the void he had left, trying hard to subdue the humiliated flush that was burning all over her body.

She was too sick at heart to try to analyze her emotions as she was driven through the rainswept night at a speed that indicated only too plainly the haste with which her companion felt compelled to rid himself of the embarrassment she had become. She sat alone in the back of the car, her unseeing eyes focused on Lian's dark head which, only a short time ago, she had dared to caress with vibrant, loving hands. She was deeply ashamed, but even in her misery she would not condemn the justice of having been made to suffer the same humiliation that he himself had suffered yesterday at her hands. She admitted that his revenge was deserved, but somewhere in the deep recesses of her mind she was wishing she could hate him for the way he had planned his deliberate punishment. But she could not hate him, because all her thoughts and energies were occupied by an even greater knowledge; the knowledge that she loved him deeply, irrevocably! Her amazed mind was grappling with this fact to the exclusion of everything else. Later, perhaps, when she could bear to relive the last incredible scene, she would plumb the lowest depths of misery, but at the present moment there was no room in her thoughts for anything other than that she loved him. Despite her mother's warnings, despite her own withdrawn, rather shy nature, she would have stayed in that primitive cottage for ever, so long as he was with her!

'Are you feeling cold?' The sharp question startled her.

'No ... no, thank you, I'm quite warm,' she stammered.

'Good!' His head swivelled back to watch the road. 'Only another half hour's drive and we'll be there.'

She peered through the window, looking for a landmark, but the summer storm had thrown a mantle of mist over the countryside and overcast skies pressed clouds low, shutting out light so completely that they were surrounded by heavy darkness. She sighed as she turned from the depressing scene, and his quick ears caught the sound.

'Don't worry,' he chided, taking her sigh to be a silent indictment of her surroundings, 'by this time tomorrow you'll be revelling in the return of your accustomed comforts, in a comfortable hotel with your own choice of companions, regaling them all, no doubt, with tales about the barbaric Irish!'

When he bit out the last savage words, her eyes filled with tears. Was there no end to the wounds this man could inflict? She had no wish to return to the brash, artificial world of business. The too few days she had spent in Kerry had shown her a side of life she had hardly known existed; a life she would jump at the chance of sharing. The idea of returning to the jungle of the boardroom surrounded by hatchet-faced men waiting, like a crowd of vultures, to pounce on any show of womanly weakness; of hastily called meetings and the shrill telephones whose noise assaulted her ears with sickening persistence, was abhorrent, and brought back in full force the weakening fatigue that had presaged her illness. She had had enough of vultures, all she wanted was to stay and breath in the pure, free air of the eagles' . . .

The car drew up with a jerk—they had arrived. Wearily she stepped out and followed him up the steps to the door. It was flung open before they reached it, and Deirdre's warm, excited voice rang out a welcome.

'Lian! Surprise! Surprise! Say you're pleased to see me!'

He bounded up the last few steps and caught the lovely laughing girl in his arms. 'When did you arrive?' he questioned, after kissing her enthusiastically. 'And how's Daniel?'

'A mere ten minutes ago, to your first question. And to your second, Father is fine, at the moment. There's to be a delay of some sort and the operation can't be performed for another week, so he begged me to return home to make sure things are being attended to as they should be. I've left him at my aunt's house until I return, the day before the operation.'

Georgina had reached the hall and was standing behind them, looking pale and shivering slightly, while she waited to be noticed. Lian's bright eyes flickered over her dejected figure and he frowned and ordered:

'Deirdre, you and Georgina go into the small sitting-room where there's sure to be a fire, and I'll go and see Kate about food and hot drinks. We can talk later.'

'Oh, Kate's promised me some supper,' Deirdre told him, 'she's just gone to prepare it.'

'Good,' Lian moved towards the kitchen quarters, 'then I'll tell her we've arrived too, she might not have heard the car.'

When they were both comfortable in armchairs set in front of a glowing fire, Georgina smiled across at Deirdre, expecting the same friendly reaction she had received from her at their first meeting, but Deirdre's beautiful face had become white and set.

'Kate told me your news,' she volunteered without a smile.

Georgina was momentarily bewildered. 'News? What news . . .?'

'The news of your engagement to Lian.' Deirdre's eyes burned as she leant forward and accused Georgina, 'I'm sorry to have to say this, because I quite liked you the first time we met: *You are not going to get away with it!*'

'Get away with it?' Georgina echoed blankly.

Deirdre drew in a deep breath. She looked magnificent in her anger as she slowly enunciated, 'Lian is mine, he's always been mine! I can't tell you for how many years I've loved him. I've waited, just biding my time until he should waken up and see me as I really am, instead of treating me like the childhood companion I was years ago. I've never really attempted to change his image of me, I felt sure it would happen gradually, given time, because not even he can remain blind for ever to the feelings I have stored up inside for him. But now you've forced my hand. You dared to think you could come here and walk away with the man I've loved all my life! Well, it won't happen, Miss Rooney, I won't allow it to happen! I give you fair warning that I intend to fight to the death for what I regard as mine—and when I say fight I don't mean passively, I mean positively, and with every weapon I have!'

And she had plenty, Georgina had to admit. Her startled grey eyes widened admiringly as she gazed back at the vivacious Irish beauty. It was just as well, she thought, that there was to be no contest; her own insignificant looks compared so dismally with Deirdre's passionate loveliness. Her lips parted to tell her how mistaken she was, but before the first word could be uttered, Lian entered the room carrying a large tray, with Kate bringing up the rear, a teapot poised in her hands.

'Ah!' There was a wealth of pleasure in the sound Kate aimed towards Georgina. 'Praise be, you've arrived back. I've just this minute been telling Himself the good news. His tenants are holding a gathering to celebrate your betrothal and it's been planned for tomorrow night. Everybody for miles around will be there, and here was I thinking you'd gone to visit with your uncle and that we'd be after having to put it off!'

No one spoke as Kate bustled forward, chattering gaily as she poured out the tea, completely unaware that her words held shattering implications for at least two of the silent people in the room.

# CHAPTER TEN

ALL the next day, Kate was immersed in preparations for the evening's 'gathering'. Georgina, when she sought her out the next morning, before breakfast, found her in the kitchen where, even at that early hour, cakes were cooling on wire racks and the spicy smell of gingerbread was drifting enticingly from the old-fashioned oven.

She had had no opportunity of speaking privately to Lian the evening before, Deirdre had monopolized his attention so unscrupulously that she had felt herself superfluous and had excused herself with a plea of tiredness and retreated to her room immediately after supper. But tired though she had been, she had woken early, with a presentiment of trouble stirring her sleepy mind into full wakefulness; a presentiment that had driven her downstairs to search for Kate in the hope that the planned celebrations could be tactfully postponed so that the ill-fated engagement might die a natural death.

But Kate's first words, spoken with happy enthusiasm, soon disabused her of that idea.

'The top of the morning to you!' she beamed. 'And a blessing on your head for giving us an excuse for a gathering.'

'Do you need an excuse?' Georgina asked weakly, certain the battle was already lost.

Kate laughed, her fine old skin crinkling into a network of delicate lace. 'Go on with ye now,' she chided, 'it's well known the Irish hate their own company so much a crowd goes to their heads like poteen! And can ye blame them?' she bristled as she prepared to defend. 'After weeks of scratching a living from an isolated smallholding with no other company than that of his wife and his livestock, is a man not justified in enjoying himself among his neighbours once in a while?'

'He is indeed,' Georgina agreed hastily, 'but I was wondering, Kate, if it would be possible to have this gathering without any mention of the engagement. After all, it hasn't been officially announced yet, and Lian might want to wait ...'

'Wait, is it!' Kate's expression of offended hauteur quickly silenced Georgina. Her mouth folded into lines of prim disapproval when she stated firmly: 'The Chief will not bring disrespect upon his name by going back on his word. Hasn't he introduced you as the future mistress of Eagles' Mount? And hasn't the whole of Kerry been told the good news by word of mouth so that there isn't a man in it who isn't itching to shake his hand and to offer you his good wishes? Why then should he want to wait?'

Georgina shook her head and backed out of the kitchen, defeated, convinced that only Lian's absolute authority would succeed in making any impression upon her argumentative victor.

She wandered disconsolately out into the grounds, so absorbed with the problem of how to avoid a public announcement of the engagement that was not that she drifted absentmindedly along a narrow overgrown path, climbing steadily upwards, becoming gradually more difficult to negotiate as its surface changed from hard-packed mud to large pebbles until finally she was clambering over miniature boulders of granite-hard rock. Somewhere below, the sea was thudding against cliffs, advancing with a boom that threatened annihilation, only to fall back frustrated with a hiss of agitated shingle to gather its forces once more.

A strong breeze whipped her slim body erect as the rough path petered out, leaving her stranded on a narrow promontory of cliff looking far out over the grey, heaving waters of the Atlantic. She drew in a quick breath when, peering over the edge, she saw seagulls in graceful flight far beneath her. Below them was a small sandy cove—a mere patch of smoothness amid the sea-strafed rocks—and on its light surface something was moving; the supple, lithe movements of a spirit at one with its raw, elemental surroundings. She dropped to her knees so that the tugging wind would not overbalance her, and levered herself cautiously forward to focus upon the solitary figure that was just beginning an ascent up the cliff face. She watched fascinated as the man picked his way along an unseen path, envying him his easy conquest of what seemed to her a sheer, rugged surface holding danger for all but its winged inhabitants to whom flight was the only safeguard from the sure death that threatened any unwary foothold.

He had almost reached the top when she recognized Lian. Her heart skipped a beat when she realized that he had been swimming; sea water still dripped down his tanned face and a damp towel was slung around his neck. She closed her eyes tightly, trying to shut out the picture of him cleaving through an antagonistic ocean, an ocean whose treacherous currents could have sucked him under and thrown him, crushed and defeated, on some alien shore or could have ripped him to pieces in the battle for supremacy between itself and the tiger-toothed rocks.

Her eyes flew open when she heard a movement, and she saw him heave himself over the edge and drop down lightly beside her. A smile quirked his lips at the sight of her fright-widened eyes, and as he searched the pockets of his black slacks for cigarettes he mocked, 'What dire foreboding shadows your peat-smoke eyes, Miss Rooney? Have you come to tell me that my house has burned down, or is it simply that you're afraid I might have forgotten my promise to take you home, and have come to remind me?'

Georgina was tongue-tied. This was their first meeting alone since last night and the shock of his rejection had, by now, had time to register. She bit her lip to subdue the longing she felt to extract a promise from him never to dare those hungry waters again, but forced herself instead to give him the answer he was so obviously waiting for as he watched her idly under half-closed lids and blew smoke rings one after the other into the silent air.

'I . . . I didn't know you were here. I was thinking and, quite inadvertently, I stumbled across the path that leads up here, and followed it.'

He deliberated for a moment, his eyes searching

her face. 'Such profound thinking?' he probed. 'About what . . . ?'

Suddenly full of anger, she met his look. He must know what it was that worried her, because surely it must also be worrying him! 'The gathering your tenants have arranged for tonight is by way of being an engagement party; we must do something to stop it!'

'Why?' He lounged back and shaded his eyes from the sun as it took a quick peep from behind banked-up cloud. She could not see his face, but his voice was as sleek as a cat stalking prey, and she shivered. Just as sleekly, he stood up and pulled her from her knees to face him. 'Why should you worry about what might be said at the gathering when, by that time, you'll be miles away?'

The touch of his hands flicked raw the nerves that had lain dormant, quivering with deprivation, since his withdrawal of the passion that had aroused them. Immediately she flinched away. The sun crept back behind the clouds, casting a frowning shadow on his face, and causing a chill in the air as he stepped back to widen the void she had placed between them.

Hastily, before he could comment on her movement, she admitted, 'We've both been rather childish, I think, but I'm tired of playing games. I have no wish to see you further humiliated, however, as you must surely be if the engagement is announced after the departure of your supposed fiancée. If you wish,' she drew herself up with small dignity, 'I'll remain here one more day, until the farce has been played out, after that you can inform 'everyone in your own good time that the engagement has been broken off.'

He pushed his hands deep into his pockets and turned to face the sea. 'That's very generous of you,' he sounded as cold and remote as the waves pounding far beneath his feet. 'So generous, in fact, that it would be churlish of me to refuse. Thank you, Gina.'

Her heart soared at the sound of this favourite name, but plummeted when common sense reminded her that its use was merely an indication of his gratitude.

'We'd better go back to the house,' she reminded him nervously, when he did not stir from his deep contemplation of the horizon. 'Kate will be waiting to serve breakfast.' And Deirdre, she silently added, will be anxious to continue where she left off last night in her campaign to make you fall in love with her ...

But he seemed in no hurry to leave. He moved closer, but did not touch her, before saying softly, 'Come here and watch the ocean.'

She was drawn to obey the soft command, and stood side by side with him watching the infinite expanse of turbulent water that was all that separated his land and her own.

'Not far from this point,' his low, musical voice told her, 'is Tralee harbour where, in days of the Penal Laws, the good ship *Jenny Johnston* used to sail for America loaded with Irish families looking for a better life and a chance to make their fortunes. We are tied by bonds of blood—your people are my people—that's why, as a wild bird is drawn to a nest it has never seen, the offspring of those early migrants come back by instinct to the nest their parents left. Do *you* feel the affinity . . .? I'm drawn back here from wherever I go. I've been in many wonderful countries and have met many beautiful women, but only one country has impressed itself upon my heart . . . and only one woman.'

He could only mean Deirdre! Georgina shook off the spell his words had cast and turned sharply to leave him, but his hand shot out to detain her. His eyes were brilliant as they silently questioned. He seemed to be looking for a sign of response, a hint of a smile, perhaps, of even a shy glance, but she kept her face expressionless, determined he would not see how much his words had hurt.

His hand dropped to his side, leaving her skin scorched where he had touched, and the tender warmth of his voice had changed to cool dryness when he finally agreed:

'You were right, we shouldn't have kept Kate waiting. Stay close behind me as I lead the way, the path can be treacherous.'

Tears blinded her as she stumbled behind his black-clad figure as he trod, sure-footed, along the path, showing in his haste his impatience to be rid of her annoying presence.

After breakfast, and at Deirdre's instigation, Lian went round to the stables to saddle two horses. He asked Georgina politely if she would care to join them, but as she had never ridden a horse in her life and, anyway, however much it hurt, she did not intend to upset Deirdre's plans by making an unwanted third on the outing that had been planned, she declined hastily. He did not press her, but by the sudden tightening of his lips she saw that he was displeased.

'Very well,' he acknowledged coldly. 'I would have thought this an excellent opportunity for you to have your first riding lesson, but if you're unwilling I won't try to persuade you. But what will you do while we're away, won't you be bored?'

'Not a bit,' she assured him, her excuse ready. 'I'll be helping Kate in the kitchen. She's promised to show me how to make soda bread and there's heaps of other things I can do to help her.'

He permitted himself a smile as he looked down at her earnest face. Her early walk had done her good, her eyes sparkled grey with—this morning—impish green flecks lighting their depths. She had chameleon eyes that stole colour from her surroundings; clear sky blue; cool grass green, or the dark grey of a troubled ocean, and he seemed fascinated by them. A wild rush of colour stained the cream of her cheeks when his gaze lingered. He traced a brown forefinger along the lines of her profile in a tender, almost absentminded way.

'How do you feel now?' His abrupt question confused her and she remained silent until he qualified, 'The dizziness that troubles you, has it gone? Are you sure you're fit enough to begin working again?'

'Oh yes, thank you,' she stammered, only then aware of how well, physically, she did feel. So much had happened to her, and so swiftly, she had had no time to think about her health, but now the question had been poised she realized she was feeling fitter than she had ever felt before. The boxes of pills which hitherto she had seldom been without lay discarded somewhere in her bedroom, and she had noticed only that morning while dressing how the waistband of her slacks hugged her much more tightly than ever it used to.

He frowned again—he had frowned a lot lately; the gay charmer she had first met could have been a dream person, so divorced was he from the present chief—and insisted: 'You are quite sure? I never again wish to see you looking as strained and over-worked as you did when you first arrived here. Obviously you need someone to take care of you, someone who will not hesitate to intercede when he sees you in danger of becoming overtired. Is there such a person?'

The question rang out like a pistol shot, demand-ing an equally swift answer, an answer she found impossible to supply.

'No, not really ... there's my mother, but she's always too busy. Besides, I don't really need any-one ...'

'Is there no one in your life who cares enough to protect you from yourself; from your insatiable thirst for work?'

Wally's face jumped to the forefront of her mind. She had almost forgotten he existed! She asked her-self the incredulous question: How could I have so completely forgotten the man I was prepared, only a week ago, to marry? But the insidious answer: Because you don't really love him! was not allowed to formulate and was thrust into the recesses of her mind before its message could disturb further

her already tattered composure.

She seized upon Wally as a lifeline, the relief of remembering his existence bringing a sudden glow to her wide eyes—a glow which did not go unnoticed by her inquisitor.

'Yes, yes ...' she babbled in her eagerness. 'There's Wally, Cassell D. Whalley. We're engaged —or almost—he's waiting until his position in the firm is established before actually asking me to marry him, but,' she swallowed painfully under his gimlet stare, 'we have an understanding.'

'So!' Lian hissed the word through lips so taut they were like slits in an expressionless mask. It echoed around the room, bouncing from the walls and seeming to increase in volume instead of being smothered amongst the heavy brocade that draped the windows and the sea of carpet that was heaving beneath Georgina's feet. She had no idea why he should be so angry, but angry he undoubtedly was; furiously angry. His fists were clenched so tightly that the knuckles showed white through the skin and his eyes glowed with a light that flickered a warning of storms ahead.

She took a step backward, alarmed by the effect her words had had upon him, and set a torch to his wrath by pleading anxiously:

'Won't Deirdre be waiting for you?'

His hands reached out to grip her shoulders with a strength that spoke of barely harnessed control while his words flayed her.

'Yes, Deirdre—you do well to mention her!' Perhaps you envy her her code of honour, the high standards she herself lives up to and which she expects from others in return? You seem to take a delight in coupling my name with hers and, who knows, perhaps I would do well to follow your directive. She, at least, would never pretend a love she did not feel simply to assuage a feeling of pique, neither would she accept the offer of a man's name and all that goes with it as an act of revenge for some imaginary slight! Yes, I might do well to look with favour upon Deirdre. She would never accept an offer of marriage from me if she were *already promised to another man!*'

He released her so suddenly that her knees buckled, and she had to grab at the nearest solid object for support. He sent a last tight-lipped look of fury across his shoulder as he flung out of the room, crashing shut the heavy oak door behind him, leaving her wilting under the force of his impetuous, bewildering resentment.

... I'm sure your mother won't enjoy tepid milk, especially when she specified that it should be hot. She'll go into the kitchen and heat up some fresh.'

Georgina swallowed hard, and sent a silent plea

# CHAPTER ELEVEN

As she dragged her heavy limbs up the stairs towards her room, Georgina heard the clatter of horses' hooves on the stone paving at the front of the house and Deirdre's gay voice as she, already mounted, chided Lian for being a slowcoach and urged him to join her quickly before the frisky mounts became beyond her control. Lian's answering voice contained none of the biting anger he seemed to reserve entirely for herself, and Georgina, as she continued up the stairs, reflected bitterly that it was just as well this was to be her last night at Eagles' Mount; she seemed to be a constant thorn in the side of the proud chief.

She no longer had any heart to join Kate in the kitchen, so for the next few hours she occupied her time packing her belongings ready for her departure the next day. Then she desultorily dusted the heavy pieces of furniture in her room and, after that, gazed out of her window at the view she had grown to love, absorbing every aspect of its majestic beauty until she was certain each detail of it was carved indelibly upon her memory.

Lian and Deirdre had not returned by lunchtime, so she ate a simple meal alone in the small sitting-room, then returned to her room to wash her hair in preparation for the evening's festivities. Later, Deirdre's light footsteps passed her door, making towards the room she had been given farther down the passage, and shortly afterwards Georgina heard the sound of running water coming from the direction of her bathroom.

Only then did she rouse herself sufficiently to begin to get ready. She was afraid of what the evening held in store, so afraid that her fingers refused to obey her commands and a lot of time was lost while she fumbled abortively with buttons and clips that simply refused to fasten. Unbelievingly, while only halfway through dressing, she heard Deirdre trip lightly past her door on her way downstairs, obviously completely ready and anxious to join Lian for a drink before setting off for the gathering.

Feverishly Georgina began to hurry. Her hair, soft with washing, refused to be confined by pins, so she had to abandon the sleek style she usually favoured and allow its dark mass to fall to her shoulders in a rippling sweep of blue lights from which fronds escaped to lie against her cheeks like newly curled feathers emerging from a fledgling's soft down. She stared into her mirror, her eyes so apprehensive that they swirled with dark grey mist, and attempted to steady her hands long enough to outline her mobile mouth with a shade of pink to match the colour of the fine wool dress she had chosen to wear. Kate had insisted that informal dress should be worn, as Lian's tenants could very well be frightened off by too much finery and might be overwhelmed by a look of sophistication. But Georgina grimaced as she looked herself over in her mirror before making her way downstairs. Kate, at least, should approve of her appearance—anyone might be forgiven for thinking her a true Gaeltach colleen, her New World sophistication had been completely dispersed, leaving her looking and feeling more timid and uncertain than any of the people she was about to meet.

But when she huried breathlessly into the room where she knew Lian and Deirdre would be waiting, she drew a breath of dismay. Deirdre was posed elegantly against a background of deep crimson curtains in an evening dress of vibrant green nylon jersey that was moulded to her curves with loving attachment. Georgian's glance swung towards Lian, who was pouring out drinks, and noted that he too was dressed formally in a dinner jacket and black tie. Too late, she realized she should have checked with him instead of accepting Kate's dictum.

Deirdre was the first to recover and her delight was evident in the way she posed the question:

'My dear, aren't you coming, then?'

Georgina's stricken eyes pleaded with Lian for understanding. 'I'm terribly sorry,' she gasped. 'Kate told me not to dress up, and as the gathering is being held in a barn I naturally thought ...' Her voice quavered into silence.

Lian's set expression did not lighten when he told her brusquely, 'It doesn't in the least matter what you wear.'

'Oh, but Lian,' Deirdre contradicted wickedly, 'you know how disappointed your tenants will be, they *expect* a show of finery. Indeed, I'd go as far as to say the women will be inconsolable ...'

Georgina crimsoned. 'I'll go and change,' she

offered wildly. 'I promise to be quick, if only you'll wait for me.'

'Nonsense!' Lian looked pointedly at his watch. 'We're late already, I refuse to delay any longer.' He put down his glass and walked towards the door which he held open, evidently determined they should both precede him. Georgina realized that he did not intend to allow further argument, so she had no option but to follow his directive and led the way, with Deirdre following, outside to the waiting car.

The barn was fifteen minutes' drive away, but sounds of merriment and laughter could be heard coming from its direction long before they actually reached the sturdily built wooden structure. Kate had told her that, as it was the only building around big enough for communal use, it had been a natural choice as the place for the tenants, *en masse*, to entertain their chief.

When the car came to a standstill outside the half-open door, a voice yelled: *'They're here!'* and to Georgina's confused eyes it seemed as if a hundred or more people cascaded through the doorway to encircle the car, laughing and crying out eager, enthusiastic welcomes. She had no time to feel shy or apprehensive because in seconds Lian and she were escorted from the car to the barn where, once inside, every one of the happy throng took it in turns to shake their hands and to offer congratulations and good wishes.

Georgina, her face flushed and her eyes bright with animation, felt ready to burst with happiness at the way Lian's people so readily took her to their hearts. That they loved Lian was obvious. The men, although chaffing him freely, accorded to him a deference given only to those who command respect, while their womenfolk's eyes, full of pride, hardly strayed from his smiling face from the moment he made his entrance. It was only when the musicians began to tune up and the crowd dispersed to form a circle around the floor that she became aware of his arm placed protectively around her shoulders. When he removed it, her quick upward glance was caught and held by him as he leant forward to inform her distantly:

'I'm afraid they're waiting for us to begin the dancing. Do you mind . . .?'

'No, of course not,' she answered stiffly.

He inclined his head, and reached out to put an arm about her slim waist. The band, who had been waiting for this signal, struck up a tune in slow waltz time and to the accompaniment of softly clapping hands they danced alone once around the floor before being joined by the rest of the dancers.

It was a heady experience to be held in his arms under the eyes of his people and to feel herself entitled, if only for a few short hours, to bask in the loyal affection they quite naturally accorded to her as their chief's future wife. It was wonderful to share in this affection, given to Lian as a reward for his devotion to his people. But their dance together was all too short. It was interrupted by a large jovial man whom Lian had earlier introduced as Tim O'Donovan, and judging from the look of triumph he threw towards his watching mates as he waltzed Georgina away in his arms, he had won the dare to

be the first to dance with the future mistress of
Eagles' Mount.

As the hectic evening advanced and the music
progressed from slow tempo to fast, Georgina surprised and delighted them all by displaying a totally
unexpected expertise in Irish country dancing.
Even she was a little surprised to find that she could
still remember the intricate steps her father and her
Uncle Michael had been at such pains to teach her
while still a mere infant, barely steady enough to
retain her balance. The lessons had ceased after her
father's death, but the skill had been so well taught
that she found no difficulty, even after a lapse of
years, in guiding her feet through the intricate
pattern of a wildly strenuous jig.

In the heady atmosphere of thumped-out, vigor-
ous music; in the applause and loudly voiced approval of her new friends, and in the unusual position
of having men almost fighting to claim her as their
partner, she was able to forget the pain of being ignored by Lian. She was even able, although it took
great effort, to manage to keep her eyes averted
from him and Deirdre, who had gravitated towards
one another immediately she had been claimed by
Tim O'Donovan. Her mind was mostly occupied
in remembering all the new faces around her: the
Murphys, the O'Regans, the O'Rourkes—names
that fell from the tongue in a swift silver stream—
and in listening over and over again to tales about
her grandfather, who was well remembered by the
elders of the community. But one small, cold section
of her brain refused to succumb to the opiate of new
experiences; it registered every frown, every smoul-

dering look Lian threw in her direction—and every warm, smiling glance he bestowed upon Deirdre.

But at least she was aware that she was a success and she, in return, loved the warm, kind country people who after a couple of hours showed plainly that they had taken her to their hearts. Whether Kate had been right in advising her not to frighten them off with too much finery, or whether the fact that they all knew and liked her Uncle Michael had any bearing upon their attitudes was hard to tell, but, by the time someone called a halt for refreshments, she knew she had been accepted, without question, as a worthy wife for their chief. Equally, she had gained an insight into Lian's people, had recognized their great endurance and lack of self-pity and had become aware, at last, of the driving force behind her uncle's determination that something should be done to ease their poverty.

Stout was flowing like water and merriment had reached its highest pitch when a man's excited voice suddenly called out:

'Glory be, look who's here! Lock up the drink before it runs dry on us, for Michael Rooney has the thirst of the divil himself!' The laughing crowd parted for an instant, and Georgina caught sight of her uncle, grinning fatuously in the doorway, obviously sure of his welcome.

'And where else would I be but at me niece's betrothal party?' he bellowed back as he started in her direction, enthusiastically shaking hands with everyone who barred his way, until he reached her side.

'So you've come to your senses?' Michael beamed

down at her, his words softly spoken to reach her ears alone. He reached out to clasp her hands in his and explained, bright-eyed, 'The news of the gathering reached me only this morning and I lost no time in getting here so no one would do me out of the privilege of making the announcement. God bless you, child, I knew all along you were your father's daughter and that your harsh words were said in a fit of passion and never really meant. Lian is a fine man, never one better, and I'll be happy to hand you over into his safe keeping.'

She was too distressed to make an immediate reply, and Michael was so intent upon making public the engagement that he failed to notice the apprehension that darkened her eyes almost to black. She made a swift gesture of appeal as he began to lead the way purposefully towards the improvised stage where the musicians sat energetically pounding out their tunes.

'No, Uncle Mike, you mustn't, please ...!' She tried to pull away from his grip, but Michael, intent upon finding Lian in the crush, would not be deterred.

'Ah, there he is!' He beckoned to Lian with his free hand and indicated his intention by gesturing towards the stage. When Lian returned a grave nod then excused himself to Deirdre, Georgina accepted the inevitable and ceased to struggle: Michael had the bit between his teeth and nothing short of an earthquake was going to prevent him from putting into words the announcement everyone was waiting to hear.

Every head turned expectantly towards them as

they mounted the stage. The music petered out and the dancers halted as the crowd on the edge of the floor surged forward, the better to hear what was about to be said. Georgina avoided Lian's eyes as they waited, one on either side of him, for Michael to begin.

'Friends, neighbours, fellow-countrymen!' was his flowery if not strictly accurate opening which, because it was spoken with such sincerity and deep feeling, was instantly forgivable. 'This, I can truthfully say, is the happiest moment of my life, the moment when I can declare to you all that your chief, Lian Ardulian, has done my niece, Georgina, the great honour of asking her to become his wife. Needless to say, she has accepted . . .'

A great roar of approval lifted to the rafters; feet stamped, shrill high-pitched whistles rent the air, and the more decorous clapped their hands in such a frenzy of delight that Georgina was moved almost to tears. As if handing over his most precious possession, Michael drew her forward to place her hand in Lian's cool clasp before stepping backward, leaving them alone together to receive the ovation that it seemed was never going to end.

Georgina's hand trembled in Lian's as wave after wave of delighted applause swept over them, making it impossible for Lian to be heard when he attempted to speak. He too seemed overwhelmed by the extent of his people's approval; his hand tightened so fiercely around her fingers they felt crushed. For the first time since the announcement, Georgina dared to look up at him and her heart fluttered, then raced quickly on, when she met his eyes and saw in them a kindling spark that looked as if it had smouldered there for hours. Even as their glances locked, the spark flamed into life. He bent his head until their lips were mere inches apart, and challenged her timidity with a mocking whisper.

'You'll have to submit to a public embrace, otherwise they'll carry on like this all night. It's expected . . .'

When she would have sheered away at the shock of his words, his hands clasped her shoulders, imprisoning her, to the delight of dozens of exultant, urging people. There was no way out. She could not give the game away by repulsing him, nor was there any action she could employ which would avert the ordeal, the prospect of which, according to her distressed eyes, he seemed to be relishing. But before she submitted, she flickered a frantic searching look over the heads of the crowd until she found Deirdre. She was standing alone and erect in a corner, her eyes fixed with anger as she waited with the rest for the expected climax. Georgina wanted to run to her with the assurance that she need not be afraid, that Lian was merely play-acting and in his teasing, mercurial way pretending to enjoy it. But there was no time. Impatient of waiting, Lian pulled her against his hard chest and breathed across her cheek just before he kissed her: 'At least try to pretend you're enjoying it!'

But when his lips claimed hers with a hard passion she found it impossible to resist, she had no need to pretend. She gave a small moan, then her arms closed around his neck and she was back again in the hay-shed hearing crazy, disjointed endearments breathed against her lips while thunder shook the ground at her feet and twin forks of lightning lit up Lian's tempest-filled eyes.

His tenants applauded wildly while they set the seal upon their betrothal, but fell silent when the doors of the barn were suddenly thrown open and two alien figures strode imperiously into their midst. Georgina, completely unaware of anyone other than Lian, was shocked into awareness when a strident American voice lashed astonished condemnation across the width of the room.

'Georgina, what on earth do you think you're doing!'

She jerked from Lian's arms like a badly manipulated puppet, and stared at the woman who was pushing her way through the crowd.

'Mother!'

She barely whispered the astonished word, but Lian drew a surprised breath and reacted quickly. Even as Stella's lips began to form angry words, he gave a signal to the band to begin playing and guided Georgina down the steps away from the curious eyes of the assembled crowd. With innate good manners, they averted their eyes from the unwelcome guests and began once more to dance, leaving Lian and Georgina to the confrontation with Stella and the man accompanying her.

Stella was furious; a slim dynamo of a woman, full of energy and zest for life, she was, for once in her life, at a loss for words. Fighting an obvious battle for control, she demanded of Georgina, 'Well, don't you think you owe us an explanation?' and for the first time Georgina noticed the man at her mother's side.

'Wally!' she uttered, confounded.

'Yes, Wally,' her mother interrupted harshly. 'He is surely entitled to know why the girl he's supposed to be engaged to is kissing another man in full view of half the population of Kerry!'

Smoothly Lian took command. 'This is no place for involved explanations, I suggest we leave for Eagles' Mount where we can continue this conversation in private.'

'Where and what is Eagles' Mount, and who are you?' Stella interrogated rudely.

Lian answered courteously, 'I am Lian Ardulian, and Eagles' Mount is my home. Georgina and her uncle have been staying with me for the past week and, if you intend remaining in Kerry, you're very welcome to join them.'

Stella's eyes flickered when Lian introduced himself and Georgina wondered if her mother had heard his name previously, but a shutter was pulled down over her tell-tale eyes before any knowledge could escape, and she was left to wonder.

Before Stella accepted Lian's invitation, her shrewd eyes clouded with suspicion. She turned to Lian and told him with dangerous softness:

'I'll go to your house, but I hardly think any explanation will be necessary. I know my brother-in-law sufficiently well to be sure there's been some dirty work afoot. It seems I may have timed my arrival well—well enough, I hope, to extricate my daughter from the clutches of her uncle and,' her hard blue eyes challenged Lian, 'his equally cunning friends!'

Lian's nostrils flared, his Celtic pride in revolt, but he quickly regained his composure and disconcerted Stella by answering quietly:

'I'll be honoured to have Georgina's mother as a guest in my house. Please follow me, the car is outside.'

# CHAPTER TWELVE

GEORGINA tried to avoid looking at Wally as the car sped them on their way to Eagles' Mount, but she could feel his reproachful eyes upon her face all during the journey. Deirdre sat between them in the back of the car, making private conversation impossible, but Stella, who was sitting up front with Lian, seemed to be making the most of her opportunity and was delivering her views in her usual forthright fashion. Georgina could not hear what was being said, but her heart sank as Lian's expression became more and more grim, and Stella's tone more and more forceful; the battle of the giants had begun. She shrank inwardly at the thought, half afraid to wonder which of the two dominant personalities would emerge the victor.

When at last they drew up in front of the house, Stella stepped from the car and looked around, giving a theatrical shiver of disgust.

'Heavens!' she jerked out with scant regard for good manners, 'how anyone could spend their lives in such a mausoleum beats me. I'll bet a thousand dollars there's no central heating . . .'

Lian did not answer, he was preoccupied, but as he led the way into the house Georgina managed a desperate whisper to Stella: 'Please, Mother, be quiet, things are not what they seem . . .' But Stella deliberately pretended not to hear and marched into the house with hostility showing in every line of her erect figure.

Deirdre, who had remained complacently silent, offered to make coffee, and left them all together in the small sitting-room where a fire glowed comfortingly warm. Georgina's eyes followed her graceful figure to the door and saw her stop to look around at the assembled company with a satisfied smile before stepping out of the room.

'And now,' Stella fixed a cigarette into an exaggeratedly large holder and waved it meaningfully towards Wally, 'I want the whole story, and I warn you both, it had better be good!' When Wally obediently rushed to her mother's side, a lighter in his eager hand, Georgina's eyes flickered towards Lian. He was watching Wally, his lips slightly curled, but he confused her by suddenly swivelling his look upon herself, his raised eyebrows and questioning look demanding an answer she was pleased she did not have to give.

'Well?' Stella rasped as she settled back against the cushions of the settee. 'I'm waiting.'

Lian rested his elbow upon the shelf of the marble fireplace and frowned down at her for a moment before beginning composedly, 'I suppose the question you want answered first is why was I kissing your daughter in front of,' he hesitated, then smiled slightly before repeating Stella's words, 'half the population of Kerry?' When Stella's hard glance confirmed this, he went on, 'Your daughter was simply doing me a favour by saving me the embarrassment of having to explain to my tenants that the engagement they had been led to believe was imminent was, in fact, non-existent. The announcement was made in good faith by your brother-in-law Michael, but Georgina and I both knew that the engagement would last for one night only, and that afterwards, when speculation had ceased, it would be allowed to die a natural death.' He held up his hand for silence when Stella would have interrupted, and surprise kept her quiet long enough for him to continue. 'It might seem to you to be a stupid thing to do, but our motives were of the best. My tenants had planned the gathering as a celebration and neither Georgina nor myself wanted to deprive them of one of the very few pleasures that are available to them. Isn't that so, Gina?'

The warmth in his voice, and his use of the diminutive, Gina, disconcerted her so much that she blushed painfully before stammering her agreement. 'Yes . . . yes, that's right.'

Wally's mouth opened, but Stella froze him to silence with a look before demanding of Georgina, 'And what about Wally, pray, did you feel no disloyalty towards him when you agreed to this idiotic plan?'

Georgina sensed Lian's tenseness as he waited with as much curiosity as the others for her reply.

'I . . . I just didn't think,' she jerked out, her face hot with colour. But then, her temper rising against her mother's censorious attitude and Wally's pained expression, 'As Wally and I are not officially engaged I felt myself free to do whatever I wished.' Out of the corner of her eye she saw Lian relax, but she had no time to dwell upon the fact. Immediately, Stella turned upon her, addressing her with the sharpness she usually employed to overwhelm opposition.

'Then it's time you were officially engaged, my girl! Perhaps then you'll knuckle down to do the job you were sent to do instead of taking off on pleasure trips, leaving important documents unsigned and costly projects incomplete. If it were not for Wally's initiative in tracing me the English deal could have fallen through, do you realize that?' she demanded harshly.

Georgina was amazed. She had never seen her mother so angry, especially not with herself. She gave the impression of being almost frightened by the outcome of her daughter's actions, which was ridiculous, Georgina thought, when she must be perfectly well aware that there was no urgency at all attached to the English deal.

Before she could retort in this vein, Lian's cold voice addressed her mother. 'Perhaps you are unaware that your daughter's health was in jeopardy and that she was acting upon her doctor's instructions when she took this holiday?'

Stella's colour rose at the vein of criticism running through his words, but true to the maxim that had stood her in good stead all her business life, she returned attack with attack.

'Ridiculous nonsense!' she challenged Lian, her hard blue eyes daring him to contradict. 'What are a few headaches and a little dizziness compared with a deal that could have lost us thousands of dollars? We American women don't cosset ourselves, Chief Ardulian, nor do we expect to be cosseted. If I'd given in to every headache I've suffered over the years there would be no Electronic International! Indeed,' she gave a hard laugh devoid of mirth, 'it was to save my daughter from suffering that I chased over here to a land in which I would never willingly set foot. I married a pseudo-Irishman, to my great sorrow, but that fate will never be allowed to over-take Georgina, not as long as I have the strength and the will to fight it!'

Lian straightened and stood tall before Stella, his jaw outthrust and his knuckles showing white through the taut skin of his clenched fists as he weathered the deliberate insult. Georgina waited, appalled, for the storm to break over her mother's head, and for once, even Stella seemed to recognize that she had gone too far. All the arrogance and nobility inherited from generations of proud Irish chieftains was reflected in Lian's face as he fought to subdue the outrage her words had aroused, and in those few seconds Georgina saw all the swagger-ing bravado drain from her mother, leaving her looking small and defenceless, like a frightened sparrow caught in the shadow of an eagle's out-stretched wings.

The unbearable tension was suddenly broken by a loud bang as the front door of the house was opened and allowed to swing back on its hinges, closing with a thud that reverberated through the house and set glasses and ornaments jingling in its draught.

Michael burst into the room, his face a study of indignation. 'Someone told me you'd left,' he charged them accusingly. Then, when he caught sight of Stella and Wally, understanding dawned.

'Ah,' he braved Stella's instant animosity without flinching, 'somehow I thought it might be you!'

'Then why aren't you chasing the next outgoing plane?' Stella questioned with cold insolence.

Michael dropped into the nearest chair, mopped the sweat from his brow, and smiled with cherubic innocence into her angry face. 'Stella, me darling, you don't really mean that,' he teased lightly. 'Sure, doesn't everyone in this room know you hold me in the greatest esteem, isn't that right now?' he appealed to the assembled company.

Miraculously, the tension that had threatened to erupt into an almighty row was dispersed by Michael's refusal to recognize it. A reluctant grin twitched at the corner of Lian's mouth as Michael's eyes beseeched Stella to meet him halfway, seemingly impervious to the contempt she was making no effort to hide. Georgina could have hugged him for timing his entrance so perfectly. Her voice was warm with feeling when she tendered an apology.

'I'm sorry, Uncle, I should have told you we were leaving, but everything happened so suddenly there wasn't time. Forgive me?'

'Think no more of it, alannah. I'm here now, that's all that matters.'

'Must you employ that dreadful accent?' Stella sounded spitefully eager to ridicule Michael. 'It's an affectation I abominate in a man as true-blooded an American as I am myself!'

'American born I may be, but my heart is here in Kerry, and well you know it!' Michael scowled back, his one vulnerable spot quivering from Stella's pitiless touch.

155

Stella shrugged. 'Then why don't you stay here permanently?' she asked with a deceptive sweetness that turned to acid with her next words. 'There's nothing to keep you in America now, no home; no close relatives . . . *and no job!*'

Michael jumped to his feet, his face puce with rage. 'I might just do that you . . . you insensible robot of a woman! Yes, I *will* do it! The only reason I've stayed so long in your employment was to keep an eye on Georgina, to help prevent her from becoming a replica of yourself. But now she's to be married to a fine young man—an *Irishman*—I feel my duty to my dead brother has been discharged and I can live my life at my own pace and in what I regard as my own country. So to the *divil* with you, Stella Rooney!' With these last volatile words, he stomped across the room and a second later the door banged to behind him, leaving in his wake a surprised breathless hush.

'Well . . .!' Stella choked, and was left speechless. Before her mother could find words to begin a tirade against Michael, Georgina broke in hurriedly:

'You must be tired, Mother, I'll see about finding you somewhere to sleep. I think Kate must still be at the gathering, but it won't take me a minute to prepare a room for you . . . and one for Wally.'

Deirdre entered with coffee just in time to hear Georgina's words. 'No need,' she offered cheerfully, 'Kate arrived back with Michael and everything is in hand. If you like, Mrs Rooney,' she smiled towards Stella, 'I'll take you upstairs. The coffee will stay hot long enough for you to have a wash, if you feel you need one?'

But Georgina had no intention of being left alone with Lian and neither did the idea appeal to Stella, because when Georgina protested: 'It's very kind of you, Deirdre, but I'll do it. You stay here and have your coffee,' she nodded in agreement, and allowed Georgina to usher her towards the door.

Only when she was safe in her mother's room, the one next to her own, did Georgina feel safe enough to expel a sigh of relief. The battle was by no means over, but this breathing space would give her time to recuperate from the almost tangible feelings of resentment and anger that had flowed in living waves between Lian and her mother. Thankful for the respite, she relaxed and began to unpack her mother's suitcase, but Stella, who was gazing thoughtfully out of the window, turned suddenly from the view Georgina loved so much and questioned her sharply:

'Michael seems to think this engagement between the Chief and yourself is genuine. Why have you not seen fit to tell him the truth?'

Georgina's grip tightened on the dress she had just lifted from the suitcase, her eyes hunted as she sought for an answer.

'He ... he was away, fishing,' she stammered. 'He heard about the gathering only this morning and rushed back to be present, so you see, there was no time to tell him.'

Stella's blue eyes hardened with suspicion. 'Are you saying that this evening was the first time an engagement had been mentioned in Michael's hearing? I'd find that hard to believe, Georgina. Michael may be a rogue, but he's nobody's fool and tonight he didn't have the look of a surprised man—more a relieved one. Are you telling me the truth?'

The dress fell from Georgina's nerveless hands as she turned away from her mother's searching eyes; it would be useless to try to deceive her, she knew that instinctively even though she had never before tried.

'*Honey!*' The change in Stella's voice was startling and Georgina reacted to its warmth like a flower to the sun. When her mother held out her arms, she rushed into them with a cry of overstrained endurance that told its own tale.

Stella stroked her hair gently as she cradled her to her breast, tightening her hold jealously when Georgina began to sob uncontrollably. Above her daughter's bent head her eyes took on a glimmer that would have been instantly recognizable to any of her competitors. 'There, there, sweetie,' she whispered, 'don't cry so, no man is worth such tears. Come, dry your eyes and tell me all about it.'

But not even to her mother could Georgina have unburdened her aching heart; not to anyone could she have borne to put into words the simple fact that she loved Lian Ardulian to distraction; that he was aware of her love, and that that love had been rejected by him in the cruellest possible way. Stella waited patiently for her to speak, but when she remained silent even after her sobbing had ceased and the tears had dried on her cheeks she bent to whisper across Georgina's bent head:

'You love him, don't you, honey?'

When Georgina stiffened, Stella went on: 'I would have done anything to have spared you this, child. I never thought, all those years ago when I was enduring the same agony, that my own daughter would one day need the condolences I received from your grandmother. She, too, knew the heartache of discovering selfishness and indifference in the heart of the man she loved. In place of the love she thought existed was a core of self-interest she found it impossible to penetrate. Oh, I don't deny that these Irishmen can be irresistibly charming—doesn't the fact that I married your father prove that?—but their charm lasts only for as long as it takes them to gain their own ends ... after that comes despair and a disillusionment that can last a lifetime.' Her arms tightened around Georgina's still figure as she urged earnestly, 'Forget him, honey, now, before it's too late! Come back to the States with me where you'll be safe, where his influence can't reach you. Work is a marvellous antidote against sorrow—believe me, *I know*!'

With a forceful finger, she tilted Georgina's chin until she could see her own image reflected in the hurt grey eyes, more troubled than the sea that pounded restlessly beneath the window. 'Promise me you'll come, Georgina, please promise me?'

Too heartsick to resist, Georgina nodded. Her eyes filled with tears of pent-up hurt, and her voice sounded husky as it was forced through a painfully tight throat.

'I'm glad you came, Mother. I needed you to straighten me out and to bring me to my senses.' Stella's heart lurched with pity as Georgina swept a strand of hair from across her eyes, the action so heavy with weariness it indicated all too clearly that she had almost reached the end of her endurance.

'I've been such a fool!' Georgina choked. 'Even though I knew he was deliberately disarming me to get me to agree to building the factory here, it made no difference to my feelings for him. Even though I knew Deirdre had first claim on him, I still allowed myself to believe he might come to love me. How could I have been so stupid?' she appealed bitterly. 'If he *had* returned my love, how could I respect a man who's content to idle away his days basking in the faded glory of times that used to be, instead of using his abilities to restore prosperity to the home he supposedly loves? His family motto is: We Dare All!' her voice cracked on a forced laugh, 'but there's one qualification that should be added—All *but endeavour!*'

Georgina was gazing blindly across the room, her thoughts too full of her own unhappiness to wonder at her mother's surprised jerk. But Stella quickly controlled herself and asked in a casual manner:

'Lian has no job?'

'None that I've heard mentioned,' Georgina shrugged despondently. 'As far as I'm aware, he spends all his time here at Eagles' Mount, daydreaming of things that might be, so full of eternal optimism that he's convinced his people, and himself, that simply wishing for a miracle will be enough to make one happen!'

Stella quickly masked the smile of triumph that flitted across her lips. Suddenly full of action, she stood up, pulling Georgina to her feet as she did so. 'That settles it!' she pronounced forcefully. 'Tomorrow morning, as early as possible, we leave for the

States. History has twice repeated itself in our family, but this time we'll be the architects of our own fate. We'll be saying goodbye to Ireland and the Irish for ever!'

But even as Georgina forced a smile of agreement, she was pondering, half fearfully, how even her dynamic, courageous mother dared throw such a challenge to the gods.

# CHAPTER THIRTEEN

STELLA had no wish for another encounter with Lian, his arrow-sharp glances made her feel uncomfortable and she hated the way his arguments seemed always so much more forceful and logical than her own; she decided to remain in her room and asked Georgina to proffer her excuses to Deirdre. 'Tell her I'm just too dog-tired to come down for coffee, honey,' she instructed as she shrugged off her dress and donned a thickly quilted dressing-gown. 'But I'd be grateful for a glass of hot milk if you can manage to scrounge one from that hawk-eyed housekeeper.'

Georgina hesitated long enough at the door to give a wan smile. 'Kate? But she's a darling, Mother, once you get to know her.'

Stella grimaced. 'I'll believe you, child, *after* you bring me up that milk.'

The dimly lighted passageway was eerily silent as Georgina made her way lightly towards the stairs. As she neared the top of the staircase, a murmur of voices coming from the hall below made her hesitate before descending. She was deadly tired, emotionally spent, and all she longed to do was to take in her mother's milk and then be allowed to creep into her own bed to sleep. So it was a desire for solitude that made her melt into the shadows, waiting for whoever it was that spoke to move away before she made a dash for the kitchen. Cautiously she craned her neck to peer downwards. The murmur of voices was still drifting up from the hall, together with something else—the whiff of a cheroot, a familiar smell that she associated with only one person. The voices grew louder and into the centre of the hall strolled Deirdre, her beautiful face serene as she walked in the shelter of Lian's protective arm. Georgina drew back as if from danger, her pulses leaping and her heart jerking rapidly against her ribs.

'Then you never intended going through with it?' Deirdre's relieved voice reached her plainly. 'Then why on earth become involved in the first place, Lian darling?' she reproached him. 'I'm astonished that you, who dislike gossip so much, should leave yourself open to speculation, especially in a matter of this kind. What on earth made you do it?'

Georgina almost gave herself away as she craned perilously over the balcony to catch his reply, but his words were too quick for her. All she saw was his dark head lower to place a fleeting kiss against Deirdre's temple, before they entered the library and the door closed firmly behind them.

Strange how a kiss had the power to please and to inflict pain at one and the same time. That Deirdre was pleased there was no doubt; her gurgle of pleasure was audible even behind closed doors, but Georgina had to close her eyes and clench her fists tightly to endure the searing ravaging hurt of it. He had been discussing her, telling Deirdre all about their bogus engagement and perhaps telling her other things, too ... She leant against the banister until the wave of hot shame that scorched through her had subsided. As she forced her shaking limbs to carry her downstairs to the kitchen she was praying silently through clenched teeth; Please, Lian, don't tell her everything ... that I almost *begged* you to make love to me ...! A sob escaped her which, soft though it was, seemed to echo around the vault-like hall, gathering momentum as it went. It bounced from the cold stone walls—clad sparsely with tattered, faded silk flags—and was tossed against the stiffly attentive suits of armour guarding the entrance. High up to the centre of the ceiling it spiralled, where it was caught up amongst shivering icicles of crystal that hung from a chandelier—thick with the dust of ages—that began tinkling delicately in unison as if, thought her fevered brain, wishing to communicate sympathy to her in her agony.

She stood immobile outside the library door, terrified to move in case the small sounds should bring Lian in search of the cause, but the door remained shut and gradually the hall regained its customary cloak of brooding silence. Nervously she bit her lip and began to move down the passage leading to the kitchen. No sound came from inside and—as Kate always sang in a repetitive chant whenever she was in residence—she breathed a sigh of relief; with luck she would get the milk and be back in her own room within the next few minutes.

But it was not to be. When she had warmed the milk and poured it into a glass set upon a silver tray, she began to make her way, hugging the shadows, back towards the stairs. Just as she reached the first step a man's voice cut through the heavy silence.

'Georgina, wait, I must speak to you!'

'Oh no,' she breathed, before turning to answer. 'Please, Wally, not now, we'll talk tomorrow, I'm so tired ...'

But when Stella was out of his vicinity Wally took on a stature of his own. 'You owe it to me, Georgina, you must realize that!' he accused.

Dully, she acknowledged that his resentment was justified and tried to clear her mind of thoughts of Lian so that she might concentrate on giving Wally all the right answers. She made no demur when he took the tray from her hands and began leading her towards the sitting-room where the fire still sent out a smouldering warmth. 'Sit here.' He guided her to a settee drawn up close to the hearth, then sat down beside her. For a moment there was silence while he decided how to begin, but once his first words were spoken the rest followed in a torrent.

'I'm not quite sure how to put this, Georgina ... How do you think I felt this evening when I walked into that shed affair and saw you kissing a complete stranger in front of all those people—*and looking as if you were enjoying it!* I know you told your mother nothing definite had been said between us, but we did have a firm understanding. You knew I wanted to consolidate my position before asking you to be my wife, and I had the impression you were quite prepared to wait. What happened, Georgina? Why did you allow Michael to take you away without first discussing it with me? I was distracted with worry when I returned to the hotel to find you'd been gone for hours and had left no forwarding address. Did you give no thought at all to my feelings?' He paused from lack of breath, his square, usually impassive features contorted with feeling. Georgina was too tired to try to explain and stared mutely back at him, willing him to understand.

Indignation filled him at her seeming lack of contrition, but then panic at the thought that there might, after all, be more to the situation than the glib Chief of Ardulian had allowed began to take precedence to the injury inflicted upon his pride. Georgina had changed even more than he had thought. At first sight that evening, he had been astonished by her lack of grooming. The primary things he admired about her were her cool composure, her exquisite good taste and sophisticated style of dress, but she could have been a cousin to any one of the simple country girls with their flushed faces, simple frocks and boisterous, uninhibited behaviour who had thronged the barn. His glance sharpened as he looked down into her troubled face; there was more than a surface change. Never had she allowed anyone to see the feelings he had only to guess lay behind the smoky-grey screen of her eyes, but now, as she looked up at him, he was disconcerted by the agony of hurt she seemed incapable of concealing.

Almost afraid of hearing her answer, he jerked out the question, 'Georgina, what does Lian Ardulian mean to you?'

There it was again, a flinching, wounded look that answered without the need of words. But he did not contradict her when she whispered, 'Nothing!

He means nothing at all to me. How could he when he has deceived me—even plotted with my uncle to use me to further his own ends?' The strain he was labouring under lessened; whether he believed her or not did not matter, he was still in there with a chance.

'Then you'll be leaving with us tomorrow?' he demanded, wanting to hear her say the words. But she was too choked to answer, and he had to be content with a jerky nod.

Lightheaded with relief, he comforted her, 'Poor darling, I'll look after you. Once we get back to the States we'll officially announce our engagement and set a date for the wedding. As your husband, I'll have the right to shoulder your burdens, and I promise you, my pet, you'll never need worry your pretty little head about another thing.'

Georgina did not answer. The warmth of the room combined with Wally's droning voice were having a soporific effect upon her tired brain. She was so exhausted she did not heed Wally's words, much less contradict them, and when his arm stole around her and he drew her head on to his shoulder she did not resist, but nestled comfortably against him and allowed her heavy eyelids to slide down over eyes shadowed with fatigue.

Mere seconds later a cold shiver feathered across her cheek, awakening her with a shudder. She looked across Wally's shoulder for the cause of the draught and paled when her eyes were caught and held by Lian's hard blue stare as he stood watching in the doorway. When Wally turned in his direction, Lian bowed and enunciated coldly:

'I beg your pardon for intruding, I wasn't aware that you were together. Mrs Rooney has been ringing her bell for the past ten minutes and when Kate answered it she ordered her to find you, Georgina, who is *supposedly*', his emphasis was slight but most noticeable, 'fetching her some warm milk. Naturally, I was concerned when Kate told me the kitchen was empty, that's why I began my search. Please excuse me for interrupting your ... conversation.'

Georgina knew immediately that under his suave manner Lian was seething with anger. His lips caricatured a smile, but she, who had experienced the charm of his spontaneous grin, knew it to be a grimace of displeasure. Displeasure that was underlined by the cold steadiness of the look that lingered on the arm placed comfortingly around her shoulders; a look fathoms deep and run through with danger. She shivered again, aware that he was displaying only the tip of his arctic displeasure, and worried in case some brash remark from Wally should pierce the brittle layer of self-control that encased his volcanic Celtic temperament.

Quickly, before Wally had overcome his surprise, she jumped to her feet and picked up the tray containing the now-cold glass of milk. 'I'll take this to my mother,' she mumbled as she brushed past him.

It was stupid of her to think that he—when in such a fiercely brooding mood—would allow her to escape so easily. His hand shot out to fasten around her wrist as she made to pass him and held her there, a prisoner, while, for Wally's benefit, he decreed smoothly:

'I'm sure your mother won't enjoy tepid milk, especially when she specified that it should be hot. We'll go into the kitchen and heat up some fresh.'

Georgina swallowed hard, and sent a silent plea for help across her shoulder to Wally. But he was oblivious to the undercurrents that flowed between them, he merely shrugged and said with a yawn:

'Then I'll get along to my room, I'm dead-beat.' He sauntered towards them on his way to the stairs and stopped to drop a perfunctory peck on her white cheek. 'Goodnight, Georgie, remember to rise early in the morning, it's a long drive and I'd like to get a good start.' With a quick nod to Lian, he sauntered on, leaving them alone together in the sombre shadowed hall that was filled with a waiting, pounding silence.

'*Georgie!*' It was hissed between Lian's teeth with a contempt that was final. With one swift movement he propelled her towards the kitchen where, once inside, their shadows cast eerie reflections against the whitewashed walls and the dull glow of a dying fire was just visible under the massive black range. He waited until she had poured fresh milk into a pan and set it to heat, before beginning his catechism.

'So you were leaving tomorrow with Wally and without a word of explanation to me?'

'But you knew I intended ...' she began, distressed by his accusing anger.

'Are you going to marry him?' he interrupted savagely, his grim profile unsoftened by the shadows. She walked across to the sink and forced her shaking hands to dispose of the unwanted milk, giving the task her undivided attention. He strode across to her, caught her shoulders in an iron grip, and swung her round to face him. 'Answer me!' he ground out, visibly aggravated by her prolonged silence.

To hide the effect his touch had upon her, she called upon the force of her own anger. 'Well, what if I am?' she challenged him, her grey eyes turbulent with an emotion she dared not let him recognize. Thrusting out a defiant chin, she defended, 'Wally is a good, kind person and he loves me, so why shouldn't I marry him?'

Lian's features tightened until the skin stretched taut across the contours of his face, a mask of icy disfavour animated only by blazing blue eyes. She stared up at him, her fright-widened eyes contradicting her brave words, then, when she felt his arms drawing her towards him, she made an abortive attempt to escape. But this was not allowed. His grasp tightened, and did not slacken until she was pulled hard against him, heart to heart and lips almost touching.

'Why not, indeed?' His breath fanned her cheek as he bent towards her. Twin flames of anger flickered deep in eyes so brilliant his look speared and frightened with its intensity. 'Why not, if, when he takes you in his arms, *like this,* your bones melt with ecstasy! If, when he looks into your eyes, *like this,* you see a promise of passion enough to set you believing you've wandered into heaven. And if,' the thrilling cruelty of his voice hardened with intent, 'you'll count the world well lost for love each time he does ... *this!*' His hard mouth swooped down and fastened upon her trembling lips in a kiss so alienly ruthless it failed completely to effect the surrender he intended. In it, she sensed panic, the panic of a man who has recognized that everything he has planned for is slipping from his clutches, and she was repelled by his utter ruthlessness. She stood passive in his arms while he tried deliberately to arouse the feelings he knew existed. Aching tears throbbed behind her lids, but were not allowed to fall—never would she give him the satisfaction of knowing that his deliberate assault upon her senses was torturing her to screaming point. His arms slackened and were withdrawn as he felt her lack of response. He lifted his mouth from her cold, unmoving lips and took a step backward, frustrated anger seething just below the surface of the reserve he donned to mask his defeat. His lips displayed a twist of mockery when he derided:

'So you intend to play for safety? With Cassell Whalley you'll never experience the heights, or the depths, just mediocrity. Are you sure that's what you want?' He was flaying himself as well as her with his tormenting words, words that flicked wounds upon her sensitive spirit she knew would never heal. 'Tell me,' he continued his diabolical inquisition, 'do you shy away from him as you do from me, or is it just a wild, barbaric Irishman who can penetrate your guard? Can only I make you forget, if only for an instant, that you're the director of a big business and make you remember that you're a woman—a warm, tender, passionate woman! If you marry Whalley you'll give up completely all your natural instincts and will become simply an automaton—living, speaking and looking like a woman, but with every feminine caprice subdued and restrained, cloaked by superficiality and meaningless sophistication so that the men you fight across the boardroom table will never guess that you're capable of weakness. Never again will you cling to a man with supplication in your eyes, and have the ache in your heart relieved by someone who understands your needs and desires ...'

'*Someone such as yourself, I suppose!*' Georgina turned on her tormentor with a fury so intense her body shook as if with ague. 'How dare you presume to know me so well—you, who only a week ago were a complete stranger to me!' Enraged by his merciless probing of wounds so tender she herself dared not disturb them, she did not stop to choose her words. 'You revel in the conceit of thinking yourself so irresistible no other man can measure up to your standards. Well, that may be so, Chief Ardulian, but there are other qualities besides an expertise in lovemaking that a woman looks for in a husband. With Wally I'll have security, companionship, mutual interests, and most important of all, reliability. I can trust Wally as I could never trust you, because whatever he does he'll do it with my interests at heart and not his own. And that's a statement I could never truthfully connect with you!'

Lian's face was clouded in shadow as her blistering indictment echoed around the room. During the long silence that followed, all the anger drained from her, leaving her with leaping pulses and a heart she felt would never know happiness again. Wounded dignity had made her attack imperative, the truth in his words had been so undeniable that she had, for shame's sake, been forced to deny them. But victory through lying is a hollow victory, and an unstable one; she knew that if he should begin again with his ruthless interrogation her flimsy fabrications would be torn to pieces.

But he made no attempt to renew his attack. Still shrouded in shadow, he pulled himself erect and answered her in a voice as bleak as the chilling Atlantic winds which even then were buffeting the old house.

'Then there's nothing more to be said, I'll wish you goodnight, Miss Rooney.' A strangled gasp of pain escaped her as he turned on his heel to leave, but this time the sound did not reach him and she was left standing, her hand held against her trembling mouth, listening to the sound of his departing footsteps as they resounded with dreadful finality upon the stone-paved floor.

# CHAPTER FOURTEEN

OUTSIDE the air-conditioned office, New York baked in the stultifying heat of an August heatwave. Georgina stood gazing out of the window, a neat pile of completed work upon her desk. She was finished, free to go, but no prospect beckoned invitingly, no interest stirred enthusiasm in her mind. Work she could cope with; even though existing in a pale grey vacuum, one detached part of her brain functioned efficiently enough to allow her to carry on with the business. But when that work was done, the whole of her mind was set free to fret and ponder; like the sensation felt by someone deprived of a limb, she was for ever conscious of her loss—of her love for Lian.

It was almost three months since she had left Ireland; three tormenting, heart-searching months during which the pain her mother had assured her would fade still pulsed through her body for the better part of each day, and for all of every night. Even now, she was thinking of Ireland as she had seen it last, the tiny patchwork fields; the expanses of purple heather mottled through with bright yellow flowering gorse; the donkeys with their panniers laden with newly gathered peat; the Gaelic name-plates atop drunken signposts and the birds—especially the birds, for nowhere, however eagerly she had sought, had she seen the majestic eagle, except at Eagles' Mount.

She was jerked rudely out of her daydream when her mother's voice reached her from across the room. She entered, waving a sheet of paper to attract attention.

'I've had a letter from Wally, honey!'

Georgina's heart sank. She hoped her mother was not going to begin pressurizing her again. But Stella was. 'He's still dreadfully unhappy about your decision not to marry him,' she began reproachfully. 'The new factory is ready to begin production—it sure was a good idea of mine to leave him in England to supervise the job—and he says that once he has set things in motion he intends coming back here to ask you to reconsider.'

'Then he'll be wasting his time,' Georgina answered with such cool disinterest Stella knew she was in the presence of the truth. 'I meant what I said, and I'll never go back on it. I can't marry Wally, ever.'

Stella frowned. Georgina's disembodied attitude was unnatural. She had been so certain that once out of the radius of Lian Ardulian's practised charm Georgina's usual lovable characteristics, her verve and natural flair, would assert themselves. But this cool, aloof stranger who looked at her through eyes too full of memories frightened her a little. She was in danger of losing her daughter and the knowledge filled her with panic. Hastily she changed the subject.

'Let's go down to the beach house this afternoon, sweetie—in fact, let's each pack a bag and spend a few days down there. What do you say, shall we play hookey?'

But the ploy to get her interest was wasted, for Georgina merely half turned from her contemplation of space and smiled apologetically. 'Sorry, Mother, I have some business to attend to. Some other time, perhaps?'

'Business? What business? There's nothing here Susan can't handle ...'

'Private business, Mother.' Georgina's tone was sharp, resentful of her mother's persistence, and Stella bit back the questions trembling on her lips. She was aware that Georgina was involved in some business deal and the knowledge that she should want to keep it from her was galling. But Stella was learning to tread warily where her daughter was concerned; to ask rather than to demand and to keep silent when every instinct urged her to question.

'Very well,' she answered with off-hand dignity, 'I'll go myself, if you won't mind being left alone for a few days?'

Georgina bit back the reply that it would be heaven, and instead she gave her mother a placating smile. 'Of course not, Mother, you go ahead, the rest will do you good. And don't you dare come back until you're good and ready, you might as well take advantage of this glorious weather.'

Not for the first time in the past three months, Stella felt herself dismissed, a feeling humbling in the extreme to one so used to doing the dismissing. With colour high in her cheeks, she left her daughter to her thoughts, aware as never before that the influence she had wielded in the past was now non-existent and that the time had come for her to begin adopting a new set of habits—habits that did not require Georgina's participation.

Georgina was still standing there half an hour later when Susan Chesterman knocked and entered the room carrying a sheaf of papers.

'Would you sign these letters, please, Miss Rooney?' Georgina turned from the window and obediently took up her pen. When her signature had been written on the last of the sheets, she instructed Susan, 'I'm expecting a Mr Drysburgh, Susan. When he arrives show him in here and then you can go. I have no further work for you today and you might as well take advantage of the weather, I know you love to sunbathe. Has my mother gone, do you know?'

'Why, thank you, Miss Rooney. Yes, Mrs Rooney left some time ago.'

Georgina sighed with satisfaction and pushed the letters across the desk towards Susan. 'Good, then I won't be disturbed.'

Five minutes later, Susan ushered in a stockily built man of medium height. He was wearing a well-cut suit, but his ruddy countenance could have labelled him a farmer, or something similar, instead of the member of the legal profession he actually was.

'Good afternoon, Mr Drysburgh,' Georgina held out her hand. 'I hope you have some good news for me?'

He shook her hand vigorously and beamed, 'I most certainly have, Miss Rooney, the best of news! Everything you suggested has gone according to plan. First of all, I contacted the United States Bureau of Commercial Fisheries, who assured me that the survey team they sent to the west coast of Ireland some years ago took an optimistic view of the prospect of building up the fishing industry there. They say there are many varieties of fish—herring, whiting, plaice, cod, haddock, lobsters, and crayfish—around the coast, as well as an increasing number of salmon in the rivers. Next, with that information in hand, I approached the frozen food firm you mentioned and, after a few lengthy discussions, they came to look favourably upon your suggestion that they might build a refrigeration plant and cannery in Kerry. This last, of course, is subject to your investing a substantial sum of money in the project.'

A frown creased his broad brow, giving him the look of a worried gnome. 'This is the only part of the scheme with which I'm not completely satisfied, Miss Rooney. Are you absolutely certain you want to invest *all* of the money left to you by your grandmother? You must realize that if you do you'll have virtually no capital left!'

'I'm quite sure,' Georgina nodded, her eyes bright with anticipation. 'Do go on with what you were saying, Mr Drysburgh.'

He shrugged, aware that her mind was made up. 'Very well, if that is what you wish.' He opened his briefcase and brought out a pile of correspondence which he leafed through while telling her, 'My next step was to contact Chief Ardulian.' Georgina's heart leapt to her throat at the mention of Lian's name, and she had to keep a firm rein on her emotions in order to concentrate on his next words. 'Needless to say, he was delighted when I outlined the proposed scheme. He assured me that the Irish Fisheries Board would be willing to help develop the industry by providing boats and gear, training schemes, and information on new fishing techniques, and that labour would present no problem as he knew dozens of families who had sons working in England who were just waiting for the chance to return home.'

Georgina broke in swiftly and Mr Drysburgh was surprised to see the glint of suppressed tears in her eyes. 'You kept your promise that my name would not be mentioned, I hope, Mr Drysburgh?' He nodded slowly, aware now that what he had suspected was true: this was no mere business deal on her part but a philanthropic action motivated by sentiment—a strange departure from family practice if all he had heard of her mother's methods was to be believed. Being possessed of a strong sentimental streak, he warmed towards her.

'You have no need to worry, I assure you, your secret is safe with me. No one but you and I will ever know who Kerry's anonymous benefactor is. Not, that is, unless at some time you wish it to be made public. However, there is one point I must take up with you. The Irish Government have insisted you must be made aware of their gratitude in a more personal manner than can be achieved by the written word, so they ask if you would be willing to receive one of their ministers who, it is proposed, will tender their thanks verbally. Would you be willing to agree to this?' When he saw signs of agitation, he anticipated her refusal and stressed, 'I would strongly urge you to accept, Miss Rooney, if only for the sake of peace. I don't know whether you are aware of it, but the Irish temperament is such that we might still be refusing them in three years' time if you don't agree to see their minister now. To you it will be a mere formality,' he reasoned, 'but to them it is an absolute necessity in the cause of good manners.'

Reluctantly, Georgina conceded his point. 'I do understand, Mr Drysburgh, and you can inform the Irish Republican Government that I shall be pleased to receive their representative whenever they wish, *provided* there is no publicity attached to his visit and that my name is used to a minimum. If they can't agree to this, I shall have to withdraw my support and, believe me, I don't want to do that.'

After Mr Drysburgh had left, she remained at her desk mulling over what he had said. He had achieved wonders in the three months since she had approached him; the plan then only half formulated in her mind. Lian had challenged her to find a way of bringing prosperity to Kerry and she believed she had done it, but without Mr Drysburgh's help she doubted if she could have achieved one half. But she wanted no thanks from Lian, she had done what she had for the people of Kerry—not just for their Chief —and she could not bear it if he should ever jump to the conclusion that her actions had been motivated by the attraction he held for her. Her head slumped down upon the desk as tears that would no longer be held back scorched down her cheeks. Sadly, it was little consolation to know that hundreds of people were to find happiness at the expense of her own.

She surfaced from her bout of misery to find the room grown dim with encroaching twilight. Apathetically she rose from her seat to make her way home. The vast army of cleaning operatives who invaded the building after working hours were busy in the empty offices, she could hear their cheery voices calling out to one another above the noise of the vacuums as they went about their work. There seemed to be an altercation going on between two of them outside her door; one wanted to enter her office and the other was trying to dissuade him against it. Thinking instructions might have been left that she was not to be disturbed, she pushed open the door to tell them the office was now available, but stepped back with a cry when she saw one of the objectors in the argument.

'Uncle Michael!' she gasped, surprise rendering her speechless.

He pushed his way past the irate cleaner with a cheery: 'There now, didn't I tell you I was her uncle?' and propelled her back into the office, closing the door firmly behind him. A thousand questions trembled on her lips during the few seconds they stared at each other, but finally all she was able to ask was:

'What are you doing here, Uncle Michael? I thought you intended staying in Ireland for good?'

Michael's eyes narrowed; instead of answering immediately he began walking jauntily around the room, picking up objects, examining them minutely, then replacing them without comment. Her taut nerves could not stand the silence. Sharply, she jogged him into replying.

'Well, Uncle Michael?'

He stopped his wandering and faced her. 'I've come to borrow some money—a large sum of money.'

Georgina quickly sat down. 'But why? What will you do with it in Ireland?'

'I've been offered the chance of a partnership in a large stud farm, Georgina, something I've always fancied. You know how much I love being around horses, and I'd pay you back every cent, honestly I would. The farm is a paying proposition—I could give you proof of that—all it needs is more capital then it'll be the best in all Ireland. I need your help, Georgina! This could bring me an interest in something that has always fascinated me as well as being security for my old age. Will you help me, advance me the money? God knows you have plenty!'

'Oh, but, Uncle Michael,' Georgina's distressed face mirrored an appeal for understanding, 'I'm terribly sorry, but it's out of the question. My money is tied up in the firm, you know that.'

He looked downcast. 'What about the money my mother left you? I understood you could draw on that?'

Georgina was in a dilemma. She desperately wanted to help him, but he must never know to what use she had put that money. 'I'm afraid I can't explain,' she told him flatly. 'You'll just have to take my word for it, I can't help you.'

Suddenly he was bending over her, laughing down into her startled face. 'No, you can't, ye spalpeen, because you've invested every spare dollar you own in Kerry, isn't that so?'

'How do you know? ... what do you mean?' she stammered.

'I suspected as much,' Michael stated triumphantly, 'but not even with my share of cunning could I find out for sure. I was damned annoyed with you for leaving Eagles' Mount the way you did, but now I think I'm beginning to understand ...' He confused her by stopping suddenly in mid-sentence and changing the subject.

'It's a fine thing you're doing, alannah,' he told her huskily, 'and I'm proud of you.'

'You tricked me!' Georgina flared. 'How could you ...!' Michael's face assumed an expression of such worried contrition that she relented. 'Oh, all right, I don't suppose it matters much now, but promise me,' she grabbed hold of his lapels and shook him in her earnestness, 'promise me you'll never tell a soul what you've found out!'

He licked his finger and drew it across his throat. 'Never,' he promised solemnly.

She did not trust the hidden laughter in his eyes, but she had to be content with his promise. When he picked up his hat and made towards the door she tried to delay him. 'Where are you going? You still haven't told me what you're doing here, and there's lots of questions I want to ask you.'

But with irritating nonchalance he waved a farewell, throwing across his shoulder as he retreated through the doorway: 'They'll keep ... until tomorrow!'

All that evening, alone in the flat she shared with her mother, Georgina pondered on her uncle's last cryptic words. Why, she wondered, did she have to wait until tomorrow for the answers to her questions? What errand had her uncle found so urgent that he could not spare her so much as a few minutes more of his time?

Those questions remained unanswered all during the next morning and halfway through the afternoon while she mechanically went through the motions of dealing with routine business. But even as she waded through piles of correspondence, she was half listening for the telephone, impatiently awaiting a call from her uncle. It rang, of course, dozens of times, but not once did Michael's cheerful voice reply when she answered.

The last call was from Mr Drysburgh. Disinterestedly, she listened while he gave her the news that the Irish Republic's Minister for Industry and Commerce had arrived in New York earlier that week and had that morning telephoned to enquire whether she would be willing to receive him and, if so, could the meeting be some time today as he had to fly back to Ireland early tomorrow morning? Her first impulse was to refuse—she wanted her day kept free for her uncle—but then good manners prevailed and she reluctantly told Mr Drysburgh to inform the Minister that she would see him at whatever time was convenient.

The next hour dragged interminably, with still no word from her uncle. It was a relief when Susan came in to tell her, in a voice full of suppressed excitement, that the Irish Minister had arrived.

'Show him in, Susan,' she answered abstractedly, her mind grappling with a problem on paper which, on any other day, would have been resolved in seconds. A few seconds later she sensed a presence in the room and looked up from her desk, straight into the startled blue eyes of Lian Ardulian! She half rose from her seat, then sank back too shocked to speak.

'*Gina!*' He too seemed shaken by their meeting. He advanced a few steps into the room. Tall, impeccably tailored, he fitted into his surroundings as if quite at home there. Her bewildered eyes noted the leather briefcase he was carrying under his arm, the soberly striped club tie and immaculate linen he was wearing, then lastly, the look of strain on his face, which was much paler than she remembered it; lips more compressed and eyes deep bitten with an emotion that could have been pain or disillusionment. She drew in a deep breath.

'Lian! What are you doing here in New York?'

Utterly perplexed, he ran his fingers through his hair, ruining its well-groomed look but, as it settled into unruly waves, making him look much more like the Lian she remembered.

'I'm here on business,' he told her. 'I was instructed to contact a Mr Drysburgh, which I did, and he informed me that I was expected at the offices of Electronic International where I would meet the person I wished to contact. Don't ask me that person's name, because I can't tell it to you; she wishes to remain anonymous. All I know of her is that she is Kerry's benefactor and we owe her a debt of gratitude it will take a lifetime to repay.'

'But I was told to expect a Minister ...' Georgina whispered.

Lian's proud head went up. 'I am a Minister, I thought you knew that. And what do you mean, *you* were expecting ...' His last few words were swallowed into a quickly indrawn breath when realization hit him. For long seconds while he grappled with the discovery he stared at her in amazed silence, then, his taut mouth relaxing into a whimsical smile, he said softly:

'I should have known, but fool that I am, I never once suspected.'

She turned her hot face away from the tenderness of his look and bravely mustered her courage.

'So this is what my uncle meant when he said I would have the answers to all my questions today?'

Lian's brow wrinkled. 'You've seen Michael? Do you mean to tell me that old reprobate knew about this and didn't tell me?'

'There are a few things he omitted to tell me, too,' she swallowed back her tears. 'That you're a Government Minister, for instance.'

There was no doubting his surprise was genuine. 'But didn't you know that when you stayed with me in Kerry? Parliament was then in recess, but I always spend my free time at Eagles' Mount. Surely someone must have mentioned it—Kate, perhaps ...?'

She shook her head, ashamed, remembering the charges she had so often laid against him. Without her realizing it, he moved and was suddenly very close. Looking down at her with a glint she could not fathom, he asked:

'Then, if you knew nothing of my work, how *did* you think I earned my living?'

The question was tendered in a tone of such deceptive gentleness she immediately stammered an answer. 'Looking after the estate ... your tenants ...'

Her explanation halted abruptly when his hands descended upon her shoulders. 'Good lord!' he accused between clenched teeth, 'you thought me a loafer, a parasite—no wonder you couldn't bring yourself to trust me!'

With an anguished sob Georgina flung away from him. 'I'm sorry,' she choked, 'but no one told me, not you, not Kate, not even Uncle Michael ...'

'I told your mother myself,' he informed her deliberately, 'the night we returned from the gathering.'

She closed her eyes the better to suffer the pain of her mother's duplicity, then whispered, 'She must have forgotten to mention it.'

He stepped closer, so that she trembled in his shadow, and asked softly, 'Does it make a difference? Will the knowledge you've gained today make it possible for you to trust me, because without trust there can't be love and,' his voice deepened, '... I need your love desperately, my darling.'

She couldn't bear it. His nearness, the warmth in his voice and the incredibly sincere meaning in his words were combining to weave a spell around her, a spell which, if she should succumb to it, could only result in her own unhappiness. Once before she had surrendered—with disastrous results. She moved away so that he would not feel the trembling that weakened her and tried to project a core of hardness into her answer.

'Love! I offered you my love once and you threw it back in my face!' A wild sob caught in her throat and at the sound of it he strode across to fold her slim, shaking body tightly in his arms. When she would have fought him, he bit out: 'Don't struggle! Relax, and lean on me.'

For all of five minutes, he silently cradled her against his heart, rocking her to and fro until the shaking and the harsh, dry sobs that racked her had ceased. Then, when he thought her calmer, he charged her with fierce tenderness, 'You little fool, don't you know when a man has reached the end of his endurance?' He bent to brush her warm cheek with his lips and whispered against her ear, 'You'll never know how much effort it cost me to refuse the sweetness you offered that night. Luckily, I recognized your innocence—your response was touching, but so inexperienced—and I would have been a swine to have taken advantage of it.' When she gave a quick, choked gasp he half smiled and carried on, 'Although it took the willpower of seven men, and I had to hurt you unbearably in the process, I managed to control my emotions and I thank God that I did! You might not have thought so then, my darling, but if I hadn't restrained myself as I did, you would have hated me for ever—afterwards.'

With her head cradled against his heart, she forced out the anguished question, 'But if you loved me then, why didn't you say so?'

'Because you didn't trust me,' he answered simply. 'I've suffered hell these past three months, wondering if I should have taken what was offered in the hope that later you might learn to trust me; calling myself every kind of fool for allowing Whalley and your mother to take you away and work their influence upon you, but what you felt for me then was not enough. Physical attraction is far removed from love; the kind of love I want from you is made up of complete trust, and even though I took the chance of losing you I had to wait until you felt that trust. Do you feel it now ...?'

The walls of ice around her heart melted, sending a flood of reawakened feeling pulsating through her body. She felt him like stone as she stood in the circle of his arms and knew he was waiting, willing her to answer. When she lifted her grey eyes to his and let him see the mute happiness mirrored there he needed no further words but pulled her closer and bent to claim her willing mouth.

Wildly her heart fluttered, as if possessed of wings, while he expertly and thoroughly demonstrated the strength of his love for her. Passionately he kissed her; her mouth, her eyes, the soft hollow of her throat, and finally her mouth again, as if unable to get his fill of its sweet generosity. She was weak with delight and delirious with happiness when she whispered:

'Can this be just a dream, Lian my darling?'

He desisted only long enough to assure her with true Celtic arrogance, 'It's no dream, mavourneen. The fantasies and nightmares have passsed, along with all the doubts and mistrust that kept us apart.' He tilted her chin to rake her face with anxious blue intentness. 'They *have* passed, have they not, my love!' He waited, wary, touchy, his quick Irish pride ready to flare at the first hint of hesitancy. She did not prevaricate by asking him specific questions. She needed no reassurance about his feelings for Deirdre, nor had she any doubts about his love for herself: he held her complete trust. Against his stern mouth, she whispered: 'Yes, they have passed . . .'

The whipcord strength of his arms tightened around her and she thrilled to the wildness of his untamed heart that was pounding beneath her cheek. His voice was ragged with feeling when he bent once more to seek her lips, saying triumphantly just before he kissed her:

'Then this is reality, mavourneen. You're here, you're mine, and I love you!'

## Golden Harlequin Library

# A Treasury of Harlequin Romances!

Many of the all time favorite Harlequin Romance Novels have not been available, until now, since the original printing. But on this special introductory offer, they are yours in an exquisitely bound, rich gold hardcover with royal blue imprint. Three complete unabridged novels in each volume. And the cost is so very low you'll be amazed!

**Handsome, Hardcover Library Editions at Paperback Prices! ONLY $1.95 each volume.**

This very special collection of classic Harlequin Romances would be a distinctive addition to your library. And imagine what a delightful gift they'd make for any Harlequin reader!

Start your collection now. See reverse of this page for **SPECIAL INTRODUCTORY OFFER!**